INTREPID BOND

MATED TO THE ALIEN UNIVERSE

DETYEN WARRIOR OUTCASTS
BOOK TWO

KATE RUDOLPH

ABOUT THE BOOK

Stalked and stranded...

All Noelle wants is some peace and time to recover. But a gorgeous blue alien can't seem to stop following her wherever she goes. His icy demeanor is enough to drive her crazy.

And his intense looks heat her up inside.

He can't stay away from the beguiling human...

Ryklin is on the edge of fixation. It's the only excuse the soulless Detyen has for his obsession with Noelle. The only way to save them both is to leave Nebula Outpost, never to return. If only he could walk away.

When they end up stranded on an abandoned planet, they'll need to rely on one another to survive.

And as Ryklin's ice thaws, nothing can stop the inferno that flares to life between them.

1

NOELLE

"Ouch!" An unseen pointy piece of metal bit into my finger, and I flinched, staring at the bright, cherry-red drop of blood as it bloomed like a jewel.

Jewels don't bloom. I had to roll my eyes at myself, and at least that made me stop scowling. My face had been stuck in one for the last hour at least. I'd been banished to the far reaches of Nebula Outpost where even the bravest feared to tread, and I hadn't seen another soul since the beginning of my shift.

The hairs on the back of my neck tingled, sending a shiver down my spine, and my jaw firmed. I refused to turn around and look down the hallway. No one would be there. They never were.

Two freaking months of jumping at every tiny

noise or surprise had me on edge. I needed to be over it by now, but my nightmares hadn't figured that out, and I'd been working on, at best, half a night's sleep every night since that *asshole* tried to make me his mate.

Damn it. There was the scowl again.

I shuddered, and then I had to set my tool down. The drop of blood was flowing down my finger now, and I needed a bandage. There was probably a medkit down the hall somewhere, but I was so close to finishing my work that I didn't want to get up, as if it might all come undone if I turned away for even a second.

There were gremlins living in the station, I would swear it.

Nebula Outpost was a big station on the edge of nowhere. We weren't part of any empire, though the Oscavians weren't *that* far away. At one point, there'd been mining down on the planet of Nebula, but a disaster ten years ago shut it down. Apparently, no one survived. I wasn't sure why they kept the Outpost running. A lot of things on our station didn't make tons of sense, but I wasn't going to question it. Maybe we were a convenient waystation for travelers. Or maybe there were just enough of us here that we paid for our own upkeep.

I was uncountable light years away from my home in the Consortium, and until two months ago, I'd never been happier.

Something clanged down the hall, and I jumped. I pressed my bleeding finger against my jumpsuit, glad the dark fabric wouldn't show a stain. My ears strained to hear if someone was coming, but it was just the everyday sounds that came from living on a space station.

It took a lot of moving parts to keep us in orbit, and sometimes those parts made metal on metal screeching noises that meant someone hadn't been doing their bit of upkeep.

He's gone, I reminded myself for the dozenth time that hour. *No one escapes penal colonies.*

Two months ago, I'd almost been killed by a madman I'd thought was my friend. He'd pointed a blaster at my head and told me all I had to do was accept him as my mate and all would be well. It was kind of hard to accept the idea of love and affection under the threat of violence, and I was sure I was dead. He'd killed before and attacked other women.

Naively, I'd trusted that station security would do their best to catch him. But if he hadn't attacked me, I was pretty sure he'd still be roaming free, smiling at me by day and murdering the innocent by night.

I sucked in a deep breath and held it for a count of three before letting it out and doing it all over again. My heart rate calmed down, but my anxiety was still there, the surety that if I let my guard down for even a second someone would take advantage and hurt me.

Maybe I needed to leave Nebula Outpost.

It wasn't the first time I had the thought. No, it had crept up on me much like a feared stalker more than a month ago, on one of the nights when I got no sleep, sure that any shadow in my rooms might be hiding someone intent on doing me harm. I'd been sleeping with the lights at full brightness, but that didn't stop my imagination from conjuring monsters.

I'd been certain I'd get over it. My best friend, Pippa, lived on the station, and leaving would mean missing her. And if I tried to go home, I'd face the shame that came from my less than ceremonious departure. But a part of me longed for the high gates and security guards of my mother's estate. No one would be kidnapping me from there.

But I'd gone willingly with my attacker at first. I

hadn't given it a second thought when he invited me to dinner.

Stupid, stupid girl.

My moping gave my finger enough time to stop bleeding, and I gathered up my tools. I only had one more set of checks to do before I could call my shift done, and it was what I'd been putting off since yesterday morning.

The maintenance closet was the furthest thing from intimidating on this ship. It was nestled between two escape pods and held some storage equipment and an access panel to some wiring that I needed to check. It would take ten, fifteen minutes tops for me to do my work.

My hands shook as I picked up my tool bag and walked towards the door.

This wasn't G-man, an incinerator on the other end of the ship that had been used as a weapon to murder one woman and attempt to kill another. Even if I got locked into the maintenance closet, I could call for help on my comm or on the communications panel on the wall. Someone would come for me in less than an hour.

But the shadows were deep in the closet. And no one could hear me scream.

Just get it over with. I had to get this done. No one else was going to be assigned to do this work, and if I missed something, some crucial part of the ship's inner workings might malfunction. What if it was life support? Or sewage? I didn't want to be responsible for that.

I opened the door, half expecting something to rush at me from inside, but the closet was empty.

There was an acrid, spoiled, musty smell that made my nose wrinkle, and for a second, I wondered if something had died in there. We didn't have rats on the station, but ships came in from all over the galaxy, and sometimes things escaped, despite the most stringent controls.

But as I got a second whiff, I realized that nothing had died. No, this was Solar Flare. The drug was cheap to make and impossible to stamp out. Station security may have not been very good at catching murderers, but that was because half of their job was taken up finding Solar Flare producers and destroying the drugs.

Or selling the stuff themselves, I had a feeling Pippa might tell me.

I pulled out my comm and approached the source of the smell. There was a small burner in the corner and a pan that was scorched black with strange streaks of bright blue and green. This looked like someone's private kitchen. A single pan wasn't big enough to produce enough Solar Flare to offset even the minimal costs of the ingredients.

Not unless artisanal, small batch poison was catching on.

I didn't touch anything. Procedure when we found spots like this was simple: record the area and report. Station security would deal with it. Or the janitorial staff.

For some reason, the mundanity of finding evidence of drug production calmed me down. It was so normal that it seemed to reset my fears. There had always been a seedy underbelly to Nebula Outpost, and I'd found dozens of sites similar to this before. It was just part of living on the station.

My ear twitched, and my head snapped toward the door just as it started to slide closed.

I lunged for it, desperate to put my fingers in its path and trigger the sensor to keep it open, but the closet was deep, and I wasn't fast enough.

Any calm vanished as the closet plunged into darkness.

I fumbled with my comm, trying to turn on the light, but my hands shook so much that I dropped it.

When I fell to my knees to search for it blindly, my fingers only felt the metal of the floor beneath me.

I'm going to die.

Was this what Pippa felt when she got locked in that incinerator?

I knew I was freaking out. I knew this was a complete overreaction to something that wasn't a big deal. But my heart threatened to beat out of my chest and sweat poured down my brow as the panic tried to sweep me away.

My breaths were choppy. I could barely drag in any air, and I felt like I was going to pass out.

I forced myself to crawl towards the door. There was a light switch, I just had to find it and turn the lights on and all would be okay. The lights should have been triggered by a motion sensor, but whoever was cooking their drugs in this little closet had probably disabled it for some unknowable reason.

Was there enough air? I couldn't breathe.

I found the door and crawled my way up. I pawed at the wall and didn't find the light switch, but I must have palmed over the sensor that opened the door. The door opened with a *whoosh,* and I stumbled out and ran into a broad chest.

I looked up, and for a second that panic rushed

back as I saw turquoise skin, short dark hair, and dark eyes.

I reeled back, but sense came rushing in a second later. My would-be murderer wasn't back from a penal colony.

The male studied me with his cold gaze. Ryklin.

The Detyen who seemed to be stalking me.

2

RYKLIN

I REACHED out to steady Noelle, my hands going to each of her biceps and holding her in place for three seconds before she tore out of my grip. Her eyes were wide, her black hair matted with sweat, and her normally light brown skin had gone pale with a sickly undertone.

"Is something wrong?" I asked. We were in Sector J, an older part of the station that was undergoing serious repairs. Everyone housed in this section had been moved to other locations, and there were warnings posted everywhere to keep out until further notice. "What are you doing here?"

She glared at me, though I didn't know why. It was a reasonable question.

I only asked reasonable questions. As a soulless Detyen, I had no motive to ask any other kind.

"I could ask you the same thing." Noelle took a few steps back and scooped her comm up from the ground. "Did you shut the door?"

"I believe there are timers on these closets." As a maintenance person, she should have known that.

Her shoulders sagged. "Right. I forgot." She nodded towards the back of the closet. "Someone's cooking Solar Flare."

It was too shrouded in shadow for me to see, but I could smell the faint hint of the drug scorching the air. "That needs to be reported."

"Yes. Obviously." She shoved her comm in her pocket. "What are you doing here?" she asked. "No one comes down here." She leaned back but hesitated before taking a step deeper into the closet.

"I was working on the greenery in the atrium of Sector J. It is my break. I decided to take a walk." The confession was my own little rebellion, though the human woman had no way of knowing that. They were words that might have once condemned me.

They *had* condemned me.

The soulless didn't need breaks. We didn't need vacation. What use were emotionless warriors if we still needed to be treated like *people*?

I couldn't take enjoyment from any of the sights on the ship, whether it was the lush greenery I helped to plant or the never-ending views of the stars around us from the viewing stations in every sector. But it was good to stretch my legs. It kept me limber, and activity kept my mind sharp.

I would give up a lot before I gave up my breaks.

"So, you just *happened* to stop in front of this closet?" Her eyes narrowed, and she crossed her arms. A combative pose.

I had studied Noelle's poses more than I should in the past two months. Longer than that, if I was being completely honest. She only crossed her arms like that when she was feeling threatened.

As if I was any sort of threat to her.

"I saw the door slide shut. I thought someone might be up to no good." And there had been something nagging at my mind, an itch deep in my brain I couldn't quite satisfy. It had me moving my feet before I could quite decide whether or not I should, and that itch had resolved the moment Noelle stumbled into me.

"Oh." Her arms uncrossed and she looked ... I wasn't sure how to describe it. Her eyes were downcast and her mouth slightly open. For a moment, her whole being had been poised for a fight, but now she looked defeated. "Screw it, I'm done for the day. I need to report this before I get any more work done." She bent down and scooped up her tools, shoving them into a canvas sack before slinging that over her shoulder.

I stepped to the side to let her exit the closet and fell into step beside her as she walked down the corridor to the lifts.

"Are you following me?" she asked, throwing me a sideways glance, lips pursed.

"I'm escorting you." It was a long walk back to maintenance headquarters. Noelle had already been put in danger once on this station. If I could prevent it from happening a second time, I would.

She picked up her pace. "I don't need an escort."

My legs were longer than hers, and I'd spent years as a trained warrior in the Detyen Legion. It took little effort to keep up. I didn't respond. She hadn't told me to leave, not technically.

Soulless Detyens were literal; we had to be. With no emotions to guide us, all we had was what we could observe, what we saw as the objective truth. There were philosophers and psychologists who might have something else to say about that, but I didn't think about them any longer.

That was the life I'd given up six years ago.

We made it to the lifts, and Noelle jabbed her finger at the call button. "You've escorted me far enough," she said. "I can take it from here." The door to the lift slid open, and she stepped in.

I joined her. "I'm taking a walk," I said. I had a full half hour for my break and escorting her would take up most of it. It was a logical use of my time.

She made a sound in the back of her throat. Frustration, perhaps. I remembered emotion, even if I couldn't feel it, and from time to time I tried to identify the unspoken evidence of it.

The rest of the walk was silent, though Noelle shot glances at me every few minutes. Finally, we arrived back at the maintenance headquarters, and she gave me a challenging look. "See, I'm fine. No stalkers but you. Now go back to work."

"Oh." I recognized the quiet, feminine voice that came from behind us and knew the sight of me caused her distress.

Pippa Vale. Drex's denya.

I turned and nodded to her in greeting as she approached the entrance to the maintenance quarters.

What she was should have been impossible. When Detyens surrendered our souls, our emotions, we gave up the hope of life, of love, of *anything* to purchase a few more years in service to the Detyen Legion. It was the darkest secret of our race, that we would give up so much, become so little, just to escape the denya price for a time.

Unmated Detyens died at the age of thirty. It was a fact of life. Before our planet was destroyed a century ago, the stories had it that there had been a robust system for identifying and connecting mates. But most of the population had been wiped out in a single, crushing blow, and the survivors were scattered across the galaxy. There were few mates to be had.

There had been no need for soulless Detyens before the destruction of Detya.

I banished the thoughts; they did me no good.

"Ryklin," Pippa said, voice steady. "What are you doing here?"

"He walked me back," Noelle replied before I could say a word, and any hostility she'd been aiming towards me seemed to have evaporated. "I found some drug evidence over in Sector J, and he happened to be passing by."

"In Sector J?" I didn't need emotions to hear the skepticism dripping from her voice.

After what I'd nearly done to her mate, I did not blame her. I held no ill will towards Drex, but I hadn't believed him when he told me he found his denya. I couldn't. I still didn't understand it, but the evidence was clear enough. The man had his emotions back. It was real.

"I'm working in the atrium, and I must return. Goodbye." As I left the two women there, I wondered if I should have said anything about Drex. I'd lived with the man for nearly five years. He may have been the closest to a friend I was able to have.

And I'd tried to kill him.

I'd been convinced that he had fixated on Pippa, that he would descend into madness and violence and endanger myself and the four other soulless Detyens on the station. Protocol dictated that the fixated needed to be terminated for the protection of all.

But I had been wrong, and Drex hadn't fixated.

I took the path back to Sector J without paying much attention to my surroundings. I must have taken a wrong turn since I ended up in front of the air lock outside of the groundskeepers' storage area on level five.

The same air lock I'd demanded that Drex jump out of and end it all.

Perhaps the soulless were a mistake.

I'd never been much for religion when I'd had my emotions. The priests of the old gods still performed their rituals, and I'd known plenty of soldiers who found comfort in it. Those priests and priestesses had reasons for the denya price, something about ancient betrayals and forgiveness, something about learning to value that which was most precious.

It made no sense. If it was anything, it was an evolutionary byproduct, something to ensure we procreated quickly but didn't have a drain on our resources.

The priests didn't want to hear such things.

I stared at the button that would open the inner door to the airlock. If the soulless were a mistake, I was one too. It would be better to remove myself from the equation before I brought more trouble down on everyone.

Or perhaps I should go and collect Zyrus, Kryin, Thalor, and Jorin to end it together.

"Ryklin?" Drex's voice cut through my thoughts, and I turned to him as if I hadn't been contemplating my own suicide.

"Drex." I studied the man. He looked the same as ever, his teal skin covered in clan markings that only peeked out from under the sleeves of his coveralls. His dark hair was shorn short, and we were the same height, though I was broader. But there was a softness to his expression now, something I hadn't seen in the years we shared quarters.

Emotion.

"Is everything alright?" he asked. His gaze flicked to the buttons that opened the airlock and then back to me. Perhaps he'd guessed the direction of my thoughts.

Or he was remembering the last time we'd stood here.

"Yes," I said. I wasn't going to jump out the airlock. Things were not so serious yet. I needed to consider it more carefully.

But I'd walked Noelle across the ship when I had no reason to do so. And I'd become distracted on my journey back. I'd be late returning to my shift.

They were signs I'd been ignoring, things I needed to consider.

There wasn't anything more to say to Drex, so I left him there with a simple nod and headed back to Sector J to finish my shift, thinking all the way.

Noelle had been on my mind for months now, and the awareness of her could turn to fixation at any moment. It was no good.

Drex may have not been fixated, but it didn't mean that I couldn't.

I had to leave the station before it was too late.

3

NOELLE

"No, stop it, that's not how you do that at all." I placed my hand over the trainee's and stopped her from breaking anything. What was the girl's name? Ursula? Uriah? I glanced down and read the hastily affixed name tag.

Orsula.

Okay. Sure.

Orsula was an eager young Oscavian who'd signed on with the half dozen other trainees this session. She was on some sort of exchange program from the Oscavian Empire and was doing her best to help. Unfortunately, she didn't seem to quite grasp which side of a screwdriver she was supposed to use.

With Fran dead and Darian ... gone, the maintenance crew was overwhelmed. It wasn't just the lack of sleep leading to my exhaustion these days. There was too much work and not enough crew to do it. The trainees should have been helpful, but Orsula was one of the more competent ones.

The gods were laughing at us.

"What am I doing wrong?" The Oscavian's pinkish cheeks went purple with a blush, and her brow furrowed in concentration.

Everything. I bit back the retort. Barely. She was here to learn, just as I'd once come here to learn. I just didn't have time to teach her. "You need to loosen this connection before you do anything. It's all in the diagram." I said it calmly. I tried to channel the monks of the Temple of Peace back home.

It wasn't working. And I couldn't take more of this.

"Head back and study your diagrams. We'll try again tomorrow." I stood before Orsula could complain.

She scurried off, head hanging low, and shoulders hunched. On another day I might have felt bad for crushing her feelings; today I was just glad she was gone.

No one was in the changing room when I got there, and I was grateful. Normally I'd chat with

Pippa, and we'd head off for dinner together or plan to hang out. But ever since she'd gotten her new boyfriend, we'd been hanging out less and less. She was working just as hard as me, and free time was beyond limited these days. I shouldn't hold it against her.

My comm beeped with a reminder that I had a call scheduled with my family in thirty minutes. I groaned.

I loved my parents, truly. And our relationship had improved immensely once I moved to a place it would take them more than a month to travel to. These calls were expensive and complicated to set up, and I tried to never miss them.

Today I just wanted to nap. Instead, I trudged back to my room and set up the equipment. Then I changed into one of my nicer dresses. It was silky and black with a rainbow of sparkly stones embedded in the material. I'd only ever worn it when calling home. On the station I basically lived in my work uniform.

The holo player came to life and projected a thirty second countdown timer hovering in the center of my room. I took a few centering breaths before taking my seat and smiling as my mother and father came into view.

The holo player made it so it almost looked like we were sitting across a table from one another. They were in front of me in three dimensions with only a slight flickering of light betraying that they were light years away.

"Noelle!" My father's face lit up, the lines around his eyes crinkling as he smiled. "You look wonderful."

"You wore that dress last time we spoke." Mother's smile was tense. Golden jewelry glittered around her neck, and she wore a white tunic, the sleeves fashioned into braids around her arms.

"I like this dress." Damn it. Of course she'd remember that. I had a handful of dresses that met my mother's standards, and I tried to cycle through them. Wouldn't want her to think I was some kind of common worker.

"She looks great, my dear." My father placed his hand on my mother's, and her expression softened. Minutely.

"Dravis's wife has given birth to their second child," was mother's next volley.

"Lovely." I had to keep my voice neutral. Dravis and I ... well, there was history there, and it wasn't exactly pretty. Mother wouldn't let me forget.

"Honey ..." Father knew what my mother was

doing, but he'd never been able to stop her when she was in a mood. And she was certainly in a mood today. Dravis's second child should have been her second grandchild, she was thinking. I should have done my duty and expanded her would be social empire.

Instead, I was a mechanic on a far-off space station.

It only got worse from there, and by the time the call ended I had a headache and my skin was itchy, like I needed to slough it off and grow a new one.

Food and then nap. It was what I needed more than anything.

I tore the dress off as soon as I could and let it pile on the floor before pulling on soft pants and a baggy T-shirt. Things were looking up. But when I approached the food processor in my prep area, the screen was blinking, and not even judicious percussive maintenance would resolve the issue.

Tears pricked my eyes, and I had to squeeze them shut. I just wanted dinner. My stomach growled. I didn't have any meal bars hidden away, and I'd eaten the last of my special snack stash the week before. If I wanted food, I'd need to head over to the mess hall.

I really didn't want to people.

But I was hungry.

Damn it.

My stomach growled again, and I glared down at my body before angrily shoving my feet into a pair of slippers and stomping over to the door. I slammed my hand down on the sensor to open it and let out a yelp of surprise when I saw Ryklin just standing there.

What did this freaking stalker want?

"Are you kidding me?" I demanded, stepping fully into the hallway and crowding his space.

Ryklin looked down at me, eyes going a bit wide. He swallowed, his throat bobbing, and looked down the hall as if he might escape my wrath.

But he was the unlucky winner of my mood. Maybe I could have held back if I'd seen him earlier in the day, but my mother's disapproval was still ringing in my ears, and my stomach was grumbling, and I just needed this day to be over. I didn't need a hulking blue alien following me everywhere I went.

"You need to stop this," I said. "You're being a freaky stalker, and it's not cool. Are you going to hold a blaster to my head and demand I accept you as my mate? I'm not going any damn place with you! Stay the hells away from me." I punctuated the glare with a firm poke at his chest.

It made my knuckle hurt.

Down the hallway, Pippa's door slid open, and she stuck her head out.

Ryklin turned away from me and held out a package that I hadn't noticed he was holding. "I discovered a few of Drex's things in the back of a drawer. Please deliver these to him."

Pippa took the pack. "Of course. Um, would you like a cup of tea?" She glanced between him and me, and I was certain she'd heard my meltdown.

My cheeks flamed. I wanted to run, but that felt like ceding ground, and my feet were rooted in place.

"No, thank you. Have a nice night." He turned and left without glancing at me. As if I didn't exist.

Pippa looked over at me. "Are you—"

"I'm fine," I snapped before she could say anything else. "Food processor broke."

"You can—"

"I'll talk to you later." I turned on my heel and stalked towards the mess hall. I'd looked like an idiot talking to Ryklin like that, and I didn't want Pippa's kind eyes or inquiring looks. No, thanks. Not tonight, not ever.

Every word I'd said to him had been justified, even if he hadn't been stalking me tonight. There'd been the other day when I didn't believe for a moment that he'd just happened down that hallway. And there'd been other times over the last two months where I'd seen him, and it wasn't a coincidence.

At first, I'd been flattered ... sort of. Or at least happy someone was looking out for me.

Now I needed him to stop. I didn't need some lumbering giant of a Detyen looking out for me. I was a big girl; I could do it myself.

That certainty was challenged when I tried to turn off my light to sleep a few hours later. My body started shaking, teeth chattering, and I was certain the door would burst open at any moment and someone would drag me away to my doom.

Maybe a lumbering Detyen protector wouldn't be so bad after all.

But none was coming. I turned my light back on and pulled my covers up. The nightmares came, as they always did. But I fought them off on my own.

I didn't need anyone's help.

4
RYKLIN

I wasn't awake. There was a strange haze to the dream world, a gauzy filter that made everything feel just a little unreal.

The soulless didn't dream. At least, we weren't supposed to.

But the world around me was evidence otherwise.

I was on the station, walking down a narrow hallway, the walls somehow leaning inward and pointing me forward. It was so dark I could barely see, but there was just enough light for me to keep stepping forward. One foot. Then another. Then another.

"Ryklin, help!" Noelle's terrified scream cut through the oppressive silence of the walkway behind me, and I ran, sprinting towards her voice. But the hallway remained the same around me, each panel of walls identical to the last.

There were no doors. No hallways.

No way out.

Noelle screamed again, and I tried to call after her, to offer her whatever solace I could. But my mouth wouldn't open, as if my jaws had been clamped shut by some outside force.

Her cries swelled in anguish, high pitched and loud enough to hurt my ears.

And then there was silence.

My feet halted, and I couldn't pick them up. I strained to hear Noelle, but there was nothing, not even the ever-present hum of the space station.

Wake up.

This wasn't real. I was in control. My neurons were firing, looking for patterns that weren't there to give my brain something to do while my body rested. It was nonsense, nothing I should be concerned with.

I still struggled against the invisible force holding me down.

Wake up.

I wouldn't let these strange thoughts torture me.

But if waking from bad dreams was a skill, I was

sorely out of practice, and I felt as caught there as an animal in a hunter's trap. My heart beat wildly, a response I couldn't control. My skin buzzed with something I couldn't define, and there was sweat on my palms.

Was this ... panic?

Even in my dream I was soulless. I could never escape the choice I'd made. So why did my body say otherwise?

A blow jolted my shoulder, and I stumbled forward for a moment before the dream dissolved around me, and my eyes snapped open in the waking world.

My roommate, Thalor, leaned over me, his hand still on my shoulder. He removed it as soon as I opened my eyes.

"Your sleep was agitated," he said. He backed up until he was sitting on his own bunk. Our bunks were twins of each other, each affixed to one wall and able to be stored flush against it when not in use to give us more space.

I wasn't sure what I should say to that. We were on high alert after what had happened with Drex two months ago. Drex may have found his denya, but it had looked very much like fixation at the time.

And I'd dreamed of Noelle.

"Thank you for waking me," I replied. "I did not realize." A lie. The soulless weren't supposed to lie. We had a strict set of rules to set our life by, and a prohibition on lying was near the top. Unless ordered otherwise, of course.

Thalor nodded and lay back down on his bed, satisfied with my answer.

I lay in the darkness for a long while before I fell back asleep. I didn't dream a second time.

When I woke, Thalor was gone. He must have had an early shift. I still had hours yet before I needed to report for duty. But though I hadn't dreamed again, my thoughts had coalesced into a certainty that washed over me as I woke.

I needed to leave Nebula Outpost today.

Whatever compulsion I had towards Noelle Kim was growing. It would only get worse until I could not control it any longer and hurt people on the station, possibly even her.

Everything in me rebelled at the thought. But that was only more evidence that the seeds of fixation were already rooted deeply within me.

I didn't know if leaving would fix it. My trainers had made it clear that fixation could not be stopped and that any fixated soulless needed to be put down. But my trainers had also said that no soulless could manage his own life, that we couldn't live without orders from a Detyen who retained his soul.

I'd been living independently for nearly five years. I suspected that there were many things my trainers didn't know. Couldn't know.

I pulled a rucksack from the closet and carefully packed it with my sturdiest clothes. I had a sufficient supply of credits in my account to take me across the galaxy. I had little to spend them on since the quarters were provided as part of my pay. They wouldn't last me forever, but I would have time to find a place.

Once my bag was packed, I pulled out my comm and sent a message to my supervisor, resigning effective immediately. Then I wrote a message for the others and set it on the middle of the small table where we ate our meals.

Thalor would see it when he came back. He would tell Jorin, Kaelor, and Zyrus. Someone would probably tell Drex eventually.

I stepped out of my quarters for the final time and headed towards the transport depot without a backward glance.

Would Noelle wonder where I went?

The thought nagged at the back of my mind, and I found my feet turning towards Sector J in a strange imitation of my dream. This was that hint of fixation again, something I should be resisting.

But one last look wouldn't hurt.

It was early. She probably wasn't even assigned to Sector J today. And if she was, her shift likely hadn't started.

But I would let myself walk there, just to try and catch one last look. And if she wasn't there, I'd walk away for good.

5

NOELLE

I DIDN'T NORMALLY work overtime. And I definitely didn't clock in this early. But my sleep had been a mess the night before, some disjointed nightmare where I called out for someone who never came.

No, not someone.

Ryklin.

Ugh. As if I needed my freaky robotic stalker invading my dreams.

And he *was* a stalker, even if he hadn't been stalking me last night. I'd seen him watching me in the halls, and he'd just *happened* to run into me more than once ever since Darian had tried to kill me. If it were Drex, I might understand. He was my best friend's boyfriend; he wanted to make sure both of us were okay.

Ryklin, though? I had no connection to the guy, and he had no reason to help.

I'd tried talking about it with Pippa once, but her face had gone stormy, and she'd said he was off-limits. She wouldn't tell me what her problem was with the guy. Apparently, it was personal between him and Drex. So, I'd stay away from the guy on friendship grounds, if nothing else.

But he wasn't staying away from me.

I had a sinking suspicion that I needed to apologize to him the next time I saw him, though. He hadn't earned the yelling last night. And I normally didn't yell.

Perversely, I kind of hoped I caught him stalking me again, just to make my yelling retroactively okay. If he stalked me today, I wouldn't need to apologize.

With that possibly insane resolution in mind, I opened the door to the utility closet in Sector J and let out a string of curses that would have made my mother blush and then send me back to etiquette classes.

The drug paraphernalia hadn't been cleared out. In fact, I was pretty sure there was more.

The closet was either low priority or someone in station security knew about it and didn't want it cleaned out. I doubted it was a sting operation to catch the culprit. And I was frustrated enough that I didn't care.

I set my bag down next to the access panel and pulled a garbage bag off the shelf beside it, carefully shoveling as much of the drug laden mess into the bag as I could, careful not to touch anything that looked especially hazardous.

Solar Flare wasn't dangerous if you touched it, though there were stupid rumors that went around saying that brushing your fingers against the stuff could send you into heart failure. I still didn't want flakes of it on my hands.

There was a trash chute at the end of the hallway and around a corner. I dragged the garbage bag behind me, wishing I had a lev-bot to make the journey easier. Sweat beaded on my brow, and I was breathing hard by the time I heaved the bag down the chute with a satisfied grunt.

Sometimes a woman had to do things for herself.

"Some asshole trashed our stuff!" A reedy voice echoed down the hallway and stopped me in my tracks just as I was about to turn the corner.

I crouched down low and slunk back, hoping no one spotted me. The door to the closet was open, and my utility bag was right there. I had my comm, and I doubted there was anything in the bag that would give away my identity. But I was only a few meters away, and they'd see me if they looked.

The hallway ended in the trash chute; there was no way out without walking past them. And I really didn't want to fight someone cooking Solar Flare.

"Do you think it was security?" The second voice was lower.

"I paid them off. I'm not an idiot," said the first.

No wonder my report hadn't gone anywhere.

If these guys saw me, they wouldn't let me go without a fight. And I had a tiny bit of self defense training, but that was all theoretical.

Fingers tight around my neck.

A blaster digging into my temple.

Bile rose in my throat. I hadn't been able to break out of Darian's hold. If I couldn't outrun these guys, they'd do whatever they wanted to me. And this deep into Sector J, this early in the morning, no one would hear me scream.

I could fit in the trash chute. Probably. Each of the chutes fed into an incinerator that ran nightly. I probably wouldn't be fried to a crisp if I ended up inside.

But I wasn't willing to risk it. Some fates were worse than being at the mercy of two drug dealers.

My gaze scrambled over everything in the hall, not quite taking in anything. Was there any weapon I could use? Anyone I could call for help?

If station security was paid off, I couldn't trust them to get here, and no one would find me before the lowlifes in the closet.

Then my eyes snagged on the escape pod on the wall opposite me.

I could hide there.

I'd have to dart across the hallway, and if they looked, they'd see me. But the voices were still arguing inside the closet, and it would only take me a second to slide inside.

It was better than sitting in the hallway and waiting to be found.

I sprang up from where I was crouched and pressed the sensor to open the door to the escape hatch. It slid open silently, and I darted inside, holding my breath as the door closed behind me.

Relief washed over me for a second, quickly followed by a sense of foreboding. Now I was trapped. If either of those guys glanced into this escape pod, they'd see me sitting inside.

This was one of the smaller pods, designed for only ten people or so to safely evacuate the ship. In the housing areas and the larger recreation areas, there were pods that could accommodate dozens and sometimes hundreds of people.

The exterior hallways were dotted with hundreds of these smaller pods so that anyone caught in a failing sector could escape without needing to run far. There were many ways the station could fail, and few of them would give us time for an orderly evacuation.

I crouched down right next to the door. There was only a small porthole that someone could look through, and I hoped they wouldn't see me. I made sure the lights stayed off and remained as still and quiet as I could, straining to hear anything.

The door was designed to withstand the vacuum of space, and I couldn't hear a single thing, cut off completely from the rest of the ship. My comm was in my pocket, and I could try and call someone now. Pippa could round up a band of engineers and clear this place out of troublemakers in an hour. But I was frozen in indecision.

By coming in early, no one knew where I was. I hadn't even bothered to check in with my supervisor before heading out to work. I hadn't wanted to deal with anyone. And now look where I was, hiding in an escape pod and hoping no one noticed me.

I was embarrassed. And I felt helpless. And I hated it.

I didn't reach for my comm.

I was just going to wait this out. The escape pods were basically part of the scenery to everyone on the ship. We passed by them every day and didn't pay any attention to them. There was no reason to think these guys might be any different. They'd walk down the hallway, see no one was there between them and the trash chute, and they'd give up.

I hoped.

Something slammed into the door.

Instinct almost had me jumping up, and I ended up clattering to the floor, falling out of my crouch when I realized exactly how stupid that would be.

Were they fighting? Did they know I was in the escape pod?

Hiding in there was a terrible idea.

I wanted to look out the porthole and figure out what was going on. If those guys figured out I was here, all they'd have to do was press a button to open the door and I'd be at their mercy.

I wasn't going to let that happen. I faced the door, ready to charge out as soon as it opened. They wouldn't expect it and maybe the element of surprise would be enough to get me past them.

I should have just run for it when I had the chance.

I could see shadows moving through the port-hole and thought there may have been three figures rather than two. Did they have another friend I couldn't see?

Judging by the thumps against the door, it was no friend.

What if I opened the door from the inside and ran out while they were distracted? It might be my best chance. Or maybe panic was making me think like a fool.

I risked a glance through the porthole but only saw a tall figure with dark hair. If there was anyone else out there, they weren't in my field of vision.

I hated being trapped. Hiding there was a terrible idea. I had to get out.

But before I could press the button to open the door, warning lights flashed, and my ears popped.

I heard a hissing sound and then lost my footing, falling backwards until suddenly I wasn't falling anymore. I was floating.

And my escape pod was hurtling away from Nebula Outpost, hurtling toward the empty planet below.

6

RYKLIN

I EXPECTED NOELLE, not two humans with greasy hair and dirty clothes whose bickering was quickly turning into a shoving match. My ear twitched, and I glanced farther down the hall just in time to see the light on the outside of an escape hatch blink once—a confirmation that the door was locked.

It shouldn't have done that with no one inside.

"Hey! Get out of here!" the human with longer hair spotted me and shouted, spittle flicking out with his words.

His taller companion took the opportunity to shove the other one out of the way. "This is our spot. Take a hike."

"Your spot?" They weren't wearing the uniforms for any of the maintenance or groundskeeping crews, and with Sector J being rehabbed at the moment, drug cookers were using all the empty corridors and closets to full advantage. "Maintenance is working in this closet."

The taller one coughed out a laugh and leaned down to pick up a canvas bag that I hadn't noticed. "Yeah? Think they're coming back soon?"

Thoughts fled as I saw Noelle's bag, and images of what they might do to her assailed me.

I charged at the humans, but they were faster than I expected. The shorter one dodged around me and kicked the side of my knee, almost sending me crashing to the floor. The taller one took the opportunity to try and punch me, but I dodged, and he didn't hit anything vital.

I grabbed his fist and twisted his arm, throwing him back into the closet. He grunted and came right back for me, and we crashed back into the hall, fists flying and bodies colliding.

He landed a lucky blow to my chin, and I had to pull back, blinking to clear my vision.

"Come on, knock him out!" the shorter one shouted.

My vision cleared, and I lunged for the short one, grabbing the collar of his shirt and slamming him against the wall. It had been years since I fought, since I used my body like the warrior I'd trained to be, and my blood pumped fast in my veins. I felt alive in a way I'd never have acknowledged if I wasn't eager to put these men down.

The soulless weren't supposed to feel eager.

At the moment, I didn't care.

We'd managed to cross half the hallway and were right by the escape hatch I'd spotted earlier. I risked a glance inside, but it was darkened, and I didn't see anyone.

Then the taller one slammed into me from behind, knocking the air out of my lungs and making me stumble forward. I released the shorter one, and he scrambled to his feet. The two of them teamed up, whatever tension had been rising earlier forgotten in the face of my threat. They wrenched me around and slammed me back until I banged against the control panel for the escape pod, and a light overhead blinked in warning.

It was preparing to launch.

One of the men cursed, knowing an unauthorized escape pod launch might bring security running. Or it might not. Security on Nebula Outpost was lacking, to say the least.

I headbutted one man and slammed my elbow into the other's guts. While turning around, I spotted something through the porthole into the escape pod.

Noelle.

Her eyes were wide and terrified, and before I could reach for the panel to stop the launch, the pod disengaged, and she went right with it, falling off the station and into the gravity field of the planet below.

After that, it wasn't a fight.

I would not let Noelle be lost to the empty land-scapes of Nebula.

The men I was fighting were decent brawlers, but they had no training. Once I truly made it my mission to neutralize them, it took less than a minute, and they were left in a groaning pile of pain as I hurled myself into the escape pod farther down the hallway and launched myself after Noelle.

It never occurred to me to call for help, to contact the station and let them know Noelle was in danger.

All I knew was that I had to save her, and it drove me forward into the unknown.

7

NOELLE

EVERYTHING HURT. I didn't know my *hair* could hurt, but as I shifted around, I swear every follicle was making itself known.

Where was I?

What happened?

The scorched smell of burning fuel and metal assailed my nose, and it all came back to me in a wave. The escape pod. The ejection.

Nebula.

So *that* was why my body hurt so much. Real gravity. I hadn't felt that in years. It pulled me down until I wanted to lie flat and let it have it's way with me. I didn't realize how different it was from the artificial stuff we had up on the station until I was experiencing it for myself.

Or maybe I'd bumped my head.

I must have passed out during my fall to land because I didn't remember a thing. The escape pods were programmed to chart a safe path for a landing on Nebula unless they were caught in the tractor field of a rescue ship. It appeared the programming still worked.

I sat up and shuddered as I realized I'd made that entire landing without being strapped in. I could have broken my neck. But I hadn't. I wanted to panic, but if I started, I knew I wouldn't stop. I had to get my bearings and figure out how I was going to get home.

This couldn't have been the first time an escape pod fell to Nebula, right? There had to be some way for the station to come and get me.

I reached for my comm, grateful it was still in my pocket, but it didn't have a signal. It was hooked into the Nebula Outpost system and not set up for further communication. The only people I talked to day to day were on the station, and when I wanted to contact my family, it was easier and cheaper to set up a relay through the station. I couldn't send a message from the ground, not from my comm.

But surely the escape pods were equipped with

radios. That was all I needed to send a distress signal.

I would have sprung into action, but it was more of a grunting crawl as I struggled to my feet and tried to ignore the way pain washed over me.

This freaking sucked.

I hoped nothing was seriously wrong with me because the chance of medical intervention was slim.

There were rudimentary controls on the pod, and I checked there for a radio. I could see exactly where it should have been. Unfortunately, all that was left were a few stripped wires. There was also supposed to be a rescue beacon, but it was gone too. I wasn't sure whose responsibility it was to do upkeep on the escape pods, but it was clearly lacking.

I wanted to scream. With no radio and no beacon, I had no way of getting a signal home. Unless ... could I somehow wire my comm to the radio transmitter—assuming that was still there— and send a signal?

Give me a wrench and point me at just about any problem on the station and I could fix it, but this wasn't anything I'd done before. I didn't deal with the complex comm systems that were required to keep Nebula Outpost in communication with the wider galaxy around us.

But how hard could it be?

Hard.

First off, I had no tools. I managed to find a small sliver of metal that I used to pry open the back panel of my comm, but I didn't know what any of the components were. And I didn't know what wires hooked into what. There was no way to connect anything. I might have managed if I had a soldering gun, but that wasn't an option.

I slumped down into the closest chair and tried not to cry.

Was I going to die down here?

A sob caught in my throat, and I tried to think of reasons I wasn't about to starve to death on a dead planet.

Pippa would notice I was gone. So would the rest of the maintenance crew. There was possibly surveillance footage in Sector J. And, if not, someone would eventually check there and realize one escape pod had launched.

There was evidence. Someone would try and look for me. Maybe my comm would give off some sort of signal they could track. Or maybe there was some way other than the beacon for the station to find the pod.

I had to hope. Otherwise, I might as well just lie down and die.

Okay. Someone would try and find me. I put that thought firmly in my mind. It had to happen. But it could take a little while.

I'd need food and water.

The emergency stores of the pod were just as ravaged as the wiring, but I found one meal bar and a small canteen filled with water. Enough for a day, maybe, and my tummy would be growling.

There was probably water outside on the planet. The mining disaster had poisoned a good portion of land, but not all of the planet, not by far. And since people didn't live there, there was a good chance that the water was drinkable.

Even better, I found a water testing stick and a small plant and animal identification kit. If I had to leave my pod, I'd at least be able to check things before ingesting them. That gave me a chance of not poisoning myself.

I needed to see where I was.

I had a vague idea of the geography of Nebula. There was a vast ocean, which I obviously hadn't landed in. The mining operation had been on the northern tip of the main continent. That continent stretched for two thousand kilometers from east to west and six thousand kilometers north to south. There was a smaller continent in the middle of the ocean, and it was mostly mountains and active volcanoes with huge lava flows and lava fields.

Saying a prayer to the gods back home that I hadn't landed on the edge of a volcano, I gathered my courage and approached the hatch, slamming my hand over the button to open the door with more force than necessary.

Sunlight nearly blinded me, and I flinched. Then, squinting against the brightness, I looked again.

No lava. In fact, the area around me was so flat it felt like I was looking out into nothingness. The ground was an intense white, which only made the sunlight brighter. But as I squinted, I could make out shapes at the very edge of my vision. Trees, maybe? Small hills? Whatever they were, they were very far away.

There was a chill in the air as I stepped out onto the hard ground. The air tasted sort of salty, and I looked around, wondering if there might have been that ocean nearby. But no, I was in the middle of a great flat expanse.

I looked up, and my eyes widened as I saw a dark shape in the sky. It was no bird.

Had Nebula Outpost already sent a rescue ship?

I used my hand to shade my eyes and tracked the progress of the small craft as it got closer and closer.

And closer. And closer.

I took off running before I could think it through.

The craft was coming in fast and headed straight for me.

8

NOELLE

THE POD LANDED in a slow sort of crash a few meters from my pod. It plowed into the dry ground and dragged on for a bit before finally stopping.

It wasn't a rescue ship. It was a pod identical to the one I'd taken, though it hadn't been treated as nicely by the atmosphere of Nebula.

My first instinct was to run toward it and offer aid. Someone was potentially in trouble, and I was more or less okay. But then I remembered the drug dealers. Had they come after me? Why would they? They didn't even know I was there.

The scuffle on the station might have ended up with someone diving into an escape pod to get away, but that was a drastic measure.

Or maybe the pod had just come loose, and it was empty, ejected by accident just as I had been.

Yeah, that was probably more likely. I tried to convince myself as I took hesitant steps closer. The pod was probably empty and might have the comm equipment that mine had been stripped of. If the rescue beacon was intact, I was saved.

Sweat beaded down my neck, and I undid the top buttons of my shirt, exposing my neck. It was getting hot, and I needed to figure out my next move. I was pretty sure you were supposed to stay as close to the area you got lost as possible so rescuers could find you, but my pod would basically be an oven in a few hours unless the temperature controls were still working.

I somehow doubted that.

I approached the second pod and braced myself as I opened the exterior door. Anyone could be in there. But who I saw didn't make any sense.

Ryklin?

He was slumped over the controls, a green trickle of viscous liquid coming out of a nasty gash on his forehead. He'd strapped himself in, but something had knocked him out.

What was he doing here?

At the moment, it didn't matter; he was better than the drug dealers. Marginally.

I climbed into the pod, and my nose wrinkled at the acrid smell. Was something burning? I didn't see any fire, but it made me move faster. I pulled the medkit off the wall and opened it, groaning when I saw that there was only a package of bandages and two small cleaning wipes.

That didn't bode well for the comms.

A tiny, possibly evil, part of me was tempted to ignore Ryklin and look at the comm situation. But the injured had to come first.

I just hoped he wasn't too injured. Basic first aid training hadn't prepared me for this.

I took one of the wipes and dabbed it against his wound, flinching in sympathy when Ryklin groaned in pain. But groaning was good. It meant he was alive. Hopefully he'd wake up soon.

I wasn't sure what I'd do if he didn't.

Distantly, I knew I was panicking, freaking out at the thought that Ryklin might not wake up. And I didn't know why. I mean, I wasn't a monster; I didn't want anyone to die on my watch. But there was this sick certainty in my guts that everything would be *wrong* if Ryklin perished.

I barely knew the guy. I didn't like the guy. But

right now, he felt like the most important thing in the world.

The bleeding had mostly stopped, and I applied a bandage. The stark white stood out against his teal skin for a moment before the color shifted to match his skin tone.

Ryklin groaned again and started to move. I put my hand on his arm to try and hold him steady, as if I could possibly stand up to his bulk.

"It's okay," I lied. "You had a bit of an accident, but you're okay. Can you open your eyes for me?" I was stroking his arm, more to comfort myself than him, the reassurance in the heat of his skin that he was still alive.

His eyes squeezed farther shut for a second before they popped open and he saw me. There must have been a strange trick of the light because I could have sworn they flashed red for a second before they went right back to their normal black.

He tried to talk but ended up coughing up dry syllables.

I reached for the water bottle I'd slipped into my pocket and held it up to his lips, carefully doling out just enough to wet his mouth and throat. "Do you know where you are?" I asked. If he'd developed sudden amnesia, we'd be in trouble.

Nothing came out when he tried to speak, so I gave him more water.

Maybe an easier question. "Do you know who I am?"

Something like anguish washed over his face. I'd never seen his expression so alive before. "Noelle." The name rasped out like I'd reached deep into his lungs and yanked away all his breath. Then he blinked and it was like nothing happened; he was as blank as ever.

Right. Okay. Moving on from *that*.

Whatever that was.

"You're in an escape pod. You crashed on Nebula. Why? What are you doing here?" The panic was still there, threading my words and trying to escape. I figured I could handle being down here alone. Somehow. Maybe. Dealing with an injured man made things about a hundred times more difficult.

And when that man was Ryklin? I didn't understand all the emotions swirling around in my gut, but I had to ignore them for now.

"I came for you," he said. "Saw you climb into the pod. Saw you get ejected. Needed to help."

"Why were you—never mind. Can you move?" Questions wanted to tumble out of my mouth, but there was no time for that, not right now. "We need to see if the comms are functioning."

With a grunt, he unbuckled his harness and stood. Somehow, that made the space half the size it had been only a second ago, Ryklin's *presence* enough to make me aware of every centimeter of him. And he had a lot of centimeters.

Part of me wanted to step back, to cede the space and regain a bit of sanity in the other part of the pod. The other part of me was determined to stand my ground. He didn't just get to show up here and take over like some conquering hero.

Though he'd look really damn good at the head of an ancient army. I wondered if he'd ever worn a kilt.

Maybe *I* was the one who'd bumped my head. It was the only way my thoughts made sense.

I squirmed my way in front of Ryklin until I could see the controls. The comms were in the same shape as they'd been in mine. The rescue beacon too.

No hope of getting a message off.

I groaned and clenched my jaw, trying not to cry.

"Check to see if there's any food or water," I told Ryklin, needing some next step. "There aren't any comms. No rescue beacon either."

He took that in stoically, of course. The man was a robot most of the time; why would this be any different?

There were two meal bars and an empty canteen.

My nose wrinkled again. "Do you smell th—" But before I could finish my question, Ryklin wrapped his hand around my forearm and yanked me towards the exit as the entire front panel burst into flames.

9
RYKLIN

THIS RESCUE WAS ILL ADVISED. And ill fated. I dragged Noelle clear of the burning craft and watched as flames engulfed it. If there'd been anything useful in the pod, there wasn't any more.

Noelle took off, and I had to run to keep up. "Where are you going?" I asked, though my voice came out louder than intended. The knock to my head had some sort of effect on me, making me feel strangely unsteady, even though my body was functional.

Her destination was clear after a moment. She arrowed straight for the door of her own escape pod, but I sped up, closing the distance between us in two strides and wrapping my arm around her waist to keep her from entering.

She struggled, but I forced myself to hold on tight. "The fire could jump that distance in a blink, and your pod will go up. Is there anything in there you'd risk your life for?"

Noelle stilled, and I let go. "That would be one hell of a jump for the fire to make," she said.

"Are you willing to risk it?" I'd seen the state of my own pod, picked over for scraps until it was barely functional. I wondered how many on the station were in just as bad condition. The escape pods would be death traps if anything catastrophic ever happened.

Her shoulders sagged. "No. There's nothing in there."

That wasn't exactly true. We could have scavenged fabric from the chairs and possibly created sacks to carry any supplies we found. There may have been other useful parts, but I refused to let Noelle risk her life when fire raged on.

"We need to move," I said. Once we were clear of both escape pods, there was little chance of the fire spreading. There was no more fuel for it. We appeared to be in some desolate depression on the planet, perhaps a dry lakebed or salt flat. Emptiness spread out in every direction, and the sun was bright overhead.

We needed shelter from that, and our only option was likely to burn up.

"We need a plan," Noelle countered. She shaded her eyes with her hand and surveyed the area around us. "Maybe there was some sort of alarm when our escape pods launched. That's the best-case scenario." I didn't need emotions to hear the doubt in her voice. "And we both have friends that will be looking for us. Someone will realize we're not on the station. Eventually. Maybe they'll find us down here."

"Your friends will be looking for you," I had to correct her before any assumptions went too far. "No one will be looking for me."

She whipped around, eyes scrunched together, and lips pressed tight. "What? Why?"

By now, Thalor must have found my note. He would have probably informed the others. "I planned to leave the station for good this morning. I resigned my position and left a note for my room-mate. He will have no reason to look for me."

She blinked a few times and then shook her head. Then she tilted it to the side. Expressions flashed across her face, but I couldn't read them. "You just planned to leave?" she stuttered out the last words, voice going high. "No goodbyes or anything?"

"I left a note," I corrected. "And I came to say goodbye to you." Clearly. If I hadn't, I wouldn't be standing here.

Her mouth opened and then closed. Then she did it again, as if she was trying to speak but couldn't find the words. "How long have you been planning this?"

Why did she care? It didn't matter, but I wanted to know how she thought, why she thought. The growing fixation in me clung to these scraps as if they were precious jewels. "I made the decision this morning, though I've been considering it for some time." I didn't mention the other option. She wouldn't understand why death might have been the kinder choice for everyone.

"So, you were just going to go and none of your friends will care?" She breathed deep, blowing out a long breath. "Never mind, that doesn't matter now. Okay, we can't depend on your friends, but Pippa will definitely realize I'm gone. And you know Pippa, she'll be looking. She'll try to find me. Us."

I did know Pippa. And if it was just me down here, there was no way she'd send anyone looking. She had a particular dislike of me, one I'd earned.

But Noelle was her best friend, and Pippa was loyal. Perhaps too loyal.

"What is your plan?" I asked. This rescue mission was suboptimal. I had acted without thinking and now was reaping the consequences. If I had taken the time to contact a rescue crew, Noelle would likely be on her way back to the ship by now, and I would be gone.

Now we were both stuck here. And she was glaring at me.

"When did you think I came up with that?" she demanded, voice harsh. "Sometime between tending to your wounds and running out of a fiery escape pod? My plan was to contact Nebula Outpost, but since some assholes stripped our pods of every bit of value, I can't do that. Can your comm reach the station?"

"No." A more complex comm hadn't been necessary. There was no one outside of Nebula Outpost for me to contact. Everyone in the Detyen Legion thought I was dead, and if they found out otherwise, I'd be executed on the spot.

"Do you have any ideas, then?" She took a step towards me, finger pointing as if she meant to poke me, but she stopped a few steps away and dropped her hand.

"We need to get in contact with Nebula Outpost. Somehow." The fires wouldn't be big enough for anyone to see from space, not unless we could make them much smokier. The black smoke threatened to choke my lungs, but it only rose a few meters in the air before it dispersed. Even if someone was looking for us, they wouldn't see that.

"Thank you for that amazing insight." She glared again and stalked a few steps north. "Between us, we have a bit of water in my canteen, your empty canteen, and three meal bars, is that right? If you were leaving, shouldn't you have a bag?"

"I dropped it when I fought the drug dealers." They had likely stolen my clothes and credit sticks as soon as they recovered from the beating I'd given them.

"You fought … Right, okay, moving on. I—"

There was a loud *whoosh* behind us, and we both whipped around to see Noelle's escape pod catch fire, eliminating our only option for shelter in the unrelenting brightness of the landscape around us.

Noelle put her head in her hands and groaned. I thought I heard her cursing, but her voice was muffled. I hadn't heard cursing like that since I was in the Legion.

"We need to move," I said. There was nothing for us here, not if we couldn't contact the station. "If we sit here and wait for a rescue, we'll die of exposure."

"I know, okay?" she snapped. "I know that. I'm trying to come up with a plan. Give me a second. Or feel free to help."

"There's probably comms equipment at the old mine." It was the only settlement on Nebula, though it had been abandoned for a decade. If we had any shot of finding equipment, it was there.

"That place is supposed to be a toxic wasteland." She took a second, holding her hand up to give her a second to think. "But it's the only option. Damn it. Okay, let's go."

It was going to be a long walk.

10

NOELLE

My feet hurt. Shoes perfect for the harsh metal corridors of Nebula Outpost weren't a match for the hard lakebed below my feet. Ryklin didn't seem to be suffering, but maybe the head injury was blocking out any foot pain.

I wished there'd been some sort of analgesic in the medkit before everything got swallowed in fire. Not for my feet, though a bit of a break would have been welcome. Ryklin's bandage was getting dark as some of the blood seeped through it. It couldn't feel nice.

But there was nothing to do about it.

We'd walked for hours, the sun slowly moving over the sky, beating down on us until I was soaked in sweat and desperate for a break. We came across a petrified bit of driftwood, and I sank down onto it. "I need a minute," I said before Ryklin could march on.

The trees were getting closer, finally. I could see the shade stretching out from their canopy, but we still had another half hour or more of walking before we reached them.

I pulled my canteen out of my pocket and swirled the bottle around. I'd poured half of my supply into Ryklin's container before we started walking, and my supply was getting low. With the heat of daylight and the long hike, my mouth was painfully dry. Still, I only took a sip. I didn't want to run out yet.

Ryklin unwrapped one of the meal bars and snapped it in half, offering one piece to me. "You need to eat," he said. "Keep up your energy."

I huffed out a bitter laugh. I was running on fumes and grit; there was no energy left. But I could manage. I was about half Ryklin's size and had to be burning less energy than him. "Eat the whole thing, you need it more." There. Good deed done.

Also, the meal bars all tasted like sawdust and old socks. It wasn't *that* much of a sacrifice.

Ryklin still held it out. "We both need calories. Eat it."

I could fight him. Not physically, but I could be stubborn about it. And then we'd be stuck here fighting until one of us gave in. And I had a sinking suspicion that Ryklin might be just as stubborn as I was.

I snatched the bar out of his hand and shoved it in my mouth, my face contorting in displeasure as the flavor hit my tongue. This one was worse than normal. Ryklin ate his like it was nothing, face placid.

I washed the taste out as best as I could, leaving only a single sip of water in my canteen.

"Let's keep going." I craved that last sip of water, both from thirst and to get the last remnants of grossness out of my mouth, but I let that temptation hang on my belt.

We had to find water soon.

It might have been easier to pass the time if we talked, but Ryklin was a moving statue beside me. He exuded an impossible calm that the situation absolutely didn't call for. We were the only two people on the planet and could die at any moment. Calm was exactly the opposite of what I was feeling.

But walking next to Mr. Statue somehow helped me clamp down on the panic.

"Oh, thank you, sweet Demeter." I picked up my

pace when we were close to the trees and rushed into the shade, letting out a groan of relief as the temperature immediately lowered by about a thousand degrees.

"Demeter?" Ryklin asked. He was slower in joining me under the leaves, eyes scanning the area for threat.

"Goddess of the harvest and a bunch of other stuff. One of the old gods back home. In the Consortium," I added as an afterthought. How would he know what my home was? "I've also heard she's a goddess on Earth." I hadn't met someone from the human homeland yet. The Consortium was made up of all sorts of people, but the humans there were mostly descended from people who'd been abducted from Earth and got abandoned along the way. It made sense we had their gods.

Ryklin just acknowledged that with a nod. "Do you know anything about life on this planet? Are there animals?" he asked.

"Some small rodents, cats, and rabbits. Nothing too big. Most of the animals were brought in by the miners. There are fish, too. Not from the miners. And," I pointed up, "trees and plants. That's most of the life here." I pulled the plant ID kit out of my pocket. "This should help us figure out what we can eat."

"We'll lose daylight soon. We need to find a place to make camp." Ryklin took the lead.

There wasn't a path in the forest, but he cleared as much as he could with his own hands. It wasn't long before a rabbit darted in front of our path, and I nearly jumped out of my skin. But the bunny was gone before I fully realized it was there.

Shadows encroached all around us. I wasn't sure how long days were supposed to be on Nebula, nights either, but I thought it was pretty human-normal. Ten to twelve hours of light followed by darkness. At least I hoped so.

With no idea when in the day we'd landed and only a vague idea of how long we'd been walking, I didn't know how much daylight we had left. And darkness would be absolute around us when night fell.

We came to a stream, and I wanted to cry with joy. Ryklin leaned back against a tree as I crouched on the muddy bank and used the water testing kit to make sure it was safe to drink. I had no idea how close we were to the mine or if the disaster there had contaminated the water. We needed to be careful.

But this water was clean.

I let some pool in my hands, the icy chill of it enough to make my fingers hurt. Then I raised my cupped hands to my lips and drank it down, uncaring that half of it ended up on my shirt.

I turned to Ryklin with a grin. "We can drink it."

His gaze was intense, eyes snagged on the strip of water that darkened the gray of my top from chest to navel. He stared for several beats before pushing off the tree and stalking towards me.

I was frozen in place as he walked closer. My heart raced, and my breath hitched. There was something electric in the air, a spark that had my nerves buzzing. I don't know if a man had ever looked at me the way Ryklin was right then. I wasn't sure if it was a good thing.

But before he reached me, he tore his gaze away and knelt at the water's edge a few meters away and filled his canteen.

I did the same. Whatever had just happened was all in my head. It had to be.

"We should make camp around here," Ryklin said. "Let's see if there's a spot where we can build a fire."

A part of me wanted to argue, wanted us to keep moving and find the mine as soon as possible. But we were losing daylight, and it would be too dangerous to move soon.

We found a clearing near the stream and gathered fallen branches that we could use for firewood. This I knew how to do. Mother and father had loved to commune with the wilderness when I was a child, and we'd spent several summer nights in the middle of the woods, sleeping under the trees and stars.

I set up a ring of stones and then came to a halt. "I don't have anything to ignite it."

Ryklin took my place and grabbed two sticks, rubbing them together with a speed and determination I don't think I could have managed. He had to be getting splinters. Or blisters. But he didn't pause.

And several minutes later, long enough that my shoulders ached in sympathy, smoke started to rise out from the sticks. It took more time, longer than I expected, for the flame to catch, and Ryklin crouched there the whole time, gently coaxing it to life.

Handy.

"Keep the flame burning," he said. "I'll hunt."

Before I could say anything about that, he was gone. I stared into the fire and wondered if this was what humans a hundred thousand years ago felt like, alone in the world and hoping for a survival that wasn't guaranteed.

That lasted for all of five minutes before I got bored. I didn't realize you could get bored while in a desperate flight for your life, but apparently you could. Or maybe I was just special.

With nothing else to do, I pulled out my comm. No signal, obviously, but there were a few games programmed into it I could play.

Then I remembered the map.

When I'd first come to Nebula Outpost, I'd wanted to learn everything there was to know about the station and its dead planet. It had been years, and I'd forgotten most of it, but I'd loaded a map onto my comm, telling myself I'd study the terrain someday.

That day was someday.

I projected the map out in front of me and tried to figure out where we were in relation to the mine. We'd walked north since we assumed we were south of it, and seeing just how far north the mine was on the map, I thought our instinct was right.

But the only landmark I had was the giant dry lakebed, and I couldn't see it anywhere on my projection.

Maybe Ryklin would have more luck.

He came back with a dead rabbit clutched in his hands. "Do you have a knife?" he asked.

How had he managed to catch dinner with no weapons? Rabbits were fast. "Did you ... How did you ...?"

"I threw a rock at it." At my blank expression, he added, "I learned many ways to hunt when I was in the military."

"You were in the military?" That explained a lot about him.

"Yes. Do you have a knife?" His tone closed off that avenue of discussion before I could think of asking more.

I shook my head. "Maybe we can sharpen a branch?" We were living the stone age life down here.

"No need. You may wish to look away. This could be messy." He took a seat beside the fire and set down the rabbit, then he flexed his hand.

And grew freaking claws.

I must have made a sound, though I didn't mean to. Ryklin looked up at me. "A knife would be more precise," he said.

Don't freak out. Don't freak out.

My weird, stoic stalker had claws. That he was using the disembowel our dinner.

Yeah, I was on the verge of freaking out.

I stared at the projection of the map while Ryklin worked. I just had to pretend this was normal. He hadn't harmed me yet. If he was a stalker, at least he wasn't a violent one. "I had a map of Nebula on my comm. When you're done with ... that ... you should take a look, see if you can orient us."

"I can show you how to read the map," he said.

"I know how to read a damn map. Just not, you know, when we're in the middle of the forest with no landmarks." What I wouldn't give for a positioning satellite at that moment.

It took a few minutes for Ryklin to finish cleaning the rabbit and getting it set up on some rocks in the fire to cook.

He studied the map for several moments, and after scrutinizing it in ways I didn't understand, pointed to a spot that looked much the same as any other. "I'm nearly certain we're near here. We need to keep heading north. Another day of walking, perhaps two, and we'll be within the mine territory. If we find an outbuilding, there may be communications equipment. It may not be necessary to make it all the way to the destruction zone."

Two days of walking for a maybe.

I let myself believe that we would find comms equipment. If I couldn't believe that, I might as well just lie down and die.

11

RYKLIN

THE FIRE PROVIDED SOME WARMTH, but it didn't make sleep comfortable. I'd survived the rugged tundra of the Detyen HQ, but Noelle shivered and scooted closer to the fire when she woke. She didn't complain, but if I had a jacket, I would have given it to her.

I didn't.

I hunted once more, and Noelle used her plant identification kit to gather some wild fruits. Flavor exploded on my tongue, tart and bright and enough to make my head ache. Soulless Detyens avoided strong tastes. The rabbit was just meat, nothing to strongly affect my taste buds. The fruit made my mouth water.

It was just hunger.

I studied Noelle's map some more and planned a path for us that I thought would be easy enough. "We'll need to pass this river soon." I pointed at the spot on the projection. "I've pinpointed a narrow spot. The water will naturally flow fast there, but we won't truly know how bad it is until we get there."

Noelle nodded and yawned, smothering it with her hand. "Do you think we'll make that crossing today?"

"Yes, in a few hours." We had the whole day ahead of us, and I didn't want to waste sunlight. "We should go."

She ended the projection on her comm and slipped it into her pocket.

I watched her as she tidied the area where she'd been sitting. She poked at the fire pit several times to make sure not even a hint of smoke rose from it. She looked over at me with a smile. "Leave the camp cleaner than you found it, that's the rule, right?"

"It's a good rule," I agreed. I couldn't look away from her. Fixation was supposed to be something violent, something terrible that would make me want to destroy.

But with Noelle I felt ... settled. Calm. Nothing

inside of me yearned for destruction—not that I could yearn at all. And if I was fixated, wouldn't I have wanted to keep her completely to myself? Our entire mission there was to find a way to communicate and get back to Nebula Outpost.

I was deluding myself. I had to be. And I couldn't even follow the sequence of logic anymore to make it make sense.

This meant trouble.

Under any other circumstances, I'd leave right then and put as much distance between us as I could. I'd already tried that, and it had only made things worse. If I hadn't engaged with those drug dealers, they might have never approached Noelle's escape pod, and she would have been able to climb out after they went away.

I was making things worse for her. I was the reason she'd fallen down to this planet.

We took off walking, and Noelle hummed a tune I didn't recognize. It was distracting and strangely calming.

It should have had no effect on me at all.

I put the concerning thoughts aside; I had to. Survival was all that mattered now.

After several hours, Noelle was making tiny sounds of suffering in the back of her throat. She didn't voice the complaints, but she must have been in pain. The gravity of Nebula was stronger than the artificial gravity of Nebula Outpost, and even I felt the strain.

"We'll take a rest here," I said. I could dimly hear the rushing of a river in the distance and didn't want to chance it without a break.

Noelle sank down onto a fallen log without protest. Her hair was plastered to her brow, and she let out a loud yawn. "This isn't anything like hiking back home."

The opening was obvious for me to pick up on it. Under other circumstances, I would have ignored it, but I suspected that she felt the need to speak, and I was the only one here to listen. "Really?"

Something in my tone must have not been correct. "If you don't want me to talk, you can just say so. I know I was annoying you with my humming earlier. It's just too quiet down here."

"You weren't annoying me." And it was, indeed, quieter than the station, but there were sounds of wildlife all around us, the wind rustling through leaves, birds chirping, and the threat of that water.

"I know when I've annoyed someone," she insisted. She rested one foot on a knee and slipped off her shoe, giving herself a feeble massage.

I dropped to my knees.

"What are you doing?" she asked, caution and alarm evident in her words.

"Your feet hurt," I said. "I can rub them better from this angle." I told myself it was the logical step, that she would walk better if she wasn't in pain. But this was not something I would have thought to offer to any of my comrades.

Noelle eyed me for a moment, but then she offered her foot. I propped it up on some fallen branches and took it in my hand.

Pain radiated up my arm so fast I couldn't stop the hiss of pain that escaped. I almost jerked back, as if I'd been hit by a blaster shot, but managed to control my response at the last moment.

Or so I thought.

"Is something wrong?" Noelle tried to pull back, but I tightened my grip on her ankle, ignoring the slice of pain.

"No," I lied.

There was no reason for this touch to hurt. There was no way it was some kind of electric shock, and even if it had been, that would have dissipated quickly. The pain faded a bit as I dug my thumbs into the arch of her foot, not completely gone, but bearable.

And the guttural sound of pleasure that came from Noelle caused a whole other kind of pain.

My head went a little fuzzy, and I had to take a deep breath as something like heat seared through me. It became my goal to cause Noelle to make another one of those noises, and then another. And by the time I pulled her other shoe off and started again on the other foot, my hands were nearly numb with pain and shaking a bit.

I didn't stop.

But I did finish, and Noelle leaned back on her log, a satisfied smile on her face. "If you ever get tired of groundskeeping, you could make a fortune offering massages."

"I don't want to touch anyone else."

It was only the truth, but Noelle looked at me as if I'd said something unforgivably strange.

"We should get a move on," she said after a long moment. She put her shoes on quickly and stood. Now there was no hint of pain in her stride, and I felt a strange sense of accomplishment in that.

The river was closer than I thought, wider too. A log and some large rocks formed a natural bridge several meters upstream, but the current around them was strong.

"Wait here," I said, grabbing the largest branch I

could find and carefully hopping from stone to stone until I was about a third of the way across. The rock was slippery, and far enough to require a bit of a jump. I crouched down and speared the branch into the water. The current jerked it out of my grasp before it hit the bottom. I retreated and returned to Noelle.

"What was that about?" she asked. She drank deep from her canteen before perching at the edge of the river to fill it back up.

"It's at least as deep as you are tall, I think. Can you swim?" Swimming from the start would be safer than falling in, though we'd need to find a way to dry our clothes.

Her face scrunched up. "Not well. And it's been a long time."

"Then we'll try the bridge. I'll go first in case anything needs to be cleared. You'll come after me. You'll need to be very careful." The current could carry either of us away before we had a chance to recover.

I climbed onto the first stone and hopped to the second. I could hear Noelle curse as she found her footing on the first stone and looked back to make sure. One of her feet was wet, but she was standing.

It was little more than a long step to the third

stone, and I waited for Noelle to make the hop to the second, braced for something to go wrong. But she landed with a wobble and shot me a slightly frantic smile.

It was becoming easier to read her expressions, but I didn't have time to puzzle out why.

The next stone was the farthest jump so far, and when I landed on one foot, my ankle tried to twist, and I came down hard on my second foot, nearly toppling into the river.

"You okay up there?" Noelle called.

"Fine." My footing was stable, and my ankle was functional. I was nearly halfway, and from there I had to step onto a log somehow lodged in the river. It wasn't particularly stable, but I didn't think my weight would dislodge it. "Wait for me to clear the log entirely before moving," I warned as I took my first step.

Noelle made it to the fourth rock with a whoop of joy. I would have looked back, but every step was treacherous. At least the next rock was close. Once I was clear, I looked back at Noelle.

She was looking at the log, brows drawn down in determination, her lips moving, though I couldn't hear her saying anything. I saw her shoulders rise and fall in a deep breath before she launched herself at the log.

She made it with a wobble, and I thought she had it. One step. Two steps. Halfway there.

Then she missed the third step, and the river rose up to swallow her.

12

NOELLE

Water.

It was everywhere, soaking streams of the current clawing at me, trying to drag me down into the depths. I sputtered, fighting against those wet hands.

Then the water was in my mouth, and my lungs burned fighting against it.

And then everything went black.

I came to on the bank of the river with lips on my mouth.

Ryklin's lips.

I didn't have a chance to think twice about it before I sputtered and started coughing that treacherous water out of my lungs. He rolled me over to my side as I heaved a hundred or so gallons of the stuff out of me, my whole body wrung out from an ordeal that could have only taken minutes.

The pats against my back turned to rubbing as I tried to regain my composure. I leaned back into the touch, savoring the contact, even if it was coming from my stalker.

Who was I kidding? Especially since it was him.

I'd never known I'd be a sucker for a foot rub, but the intensity he'd shown there had given me ideas. If the man could turn me into a purring pile of goo from that, what could he do with the rest of his body?

Clearly this planet was making me crazy when it wasn't trying to kill me.

I sat up, and Ryklin's hand fell away.

"How are you feeling?" he asked. He sounded the same as ever, blank and uncaring, but I could still feel the phantom of his touch.

"Like a drowned rat." I shivered, and it wasn't an act. "I'm sorry."

"You have nothing to apologize for." He stood and offered me a hand.

I took it and noticed his flinch. He kept doing that. First with the foot rub and now this. But I was sure if I asked, he'd say nothing about it. I was coming to understand Ryklin, and he liked to play things close to his chest.

Fine. I wouldn't give him the satisfaction of asking.

We were on the bank of the river in the shade of the trees, and it was freaking freezing. I couldn't stop the shiver that wracked my body or the way my teeth chattered. And the sun would be setting soon. This was only going to get worse.

"We need to keep moving," I tried to say past my clinking teeth. I'm not sure which words came out. I wanted to cross more distance, to get closer to the mine.

I wanted to go home.

"We need to get dry," Ryklin countered. "Over there." He pointed to a patch of beach not shaded by trees. There were flat stones soaking up the sun and they might just be warm enough to keep the hypothermia at bay.

I didn't want to surrender a single item of cloth-ing, but I knew I couldn't get my socks or shoes dry without taking them off. My pants were a thick fabric meant to resist tears and stains from my work, and luckily, they were water resistant. My shirt? Not so much. Still, I left it on.

"You'll warm up faster if you take off the shirt,"

Ryklin said as he stripped off his own shirt and pants and laid them out on the rock next to us.

I wasn't going to look. I couldn't look. I had to look.

Oh, stars above.

Hells below.

Damn.

Ryklin's body made me want to drool. Muscle rippled beneath his skin, and I thought I saw scars, but my eyes snagged on his pecs and the hard planes of his abs. He had a dusting of dark hair on his chest, and it trailed down his stomach in a teasing line that disappeared into his underwear. His skin was a vibrant teal dotted with dark markings, almost like some sort of big cat from ancient Earth.

My fingers ached to touch. I was probably staring.

Why couldn't I look away?

"Is something wrong?" he asked after several moments.

Who was the creepy stalker now?

I tore my gaze away. "I bet you'd like it if I took my shirt off."

"It would be optimal if you warmed up faster." How could he still sound so calm after all that? He was standing there practically naked like nothing mattered!

"Are you a fucking robot or something? You're ... You're ... I just fell in the freaking river, and you're standing there naked like it's nothing!" I made the mistake of looking at him again, and if I wasn't so pissed off, I might want to touch.

No, that was a lie.

I was pissed off *and* I wanted to touch.

Ryklin was silent for several beats. "If you let your top dry, I will tell you," he bargained.

This was a ploy. It had to be. But somehow my shirt felt even wetter after hanging on me for the last few minutes, and I realized that water dripping off of it was starting to soak the waistband of my pants. I didn't let myself think about it before I tore the shirt off and laid it out beside my shoes and socks.

My bra wasn't dry, but Ryklin would have to tear it off me if he wanted it gone.

Not that there wasn't appeal in that thought.

No. Bad Noelle. Stop thinking naughty thoughts.

Ryklin settled down on the rock and lay back, soaking up the sun. I tried to judge its position in the sky and was pretty sure we were losing daylight fast.

We'd been walking for hours. I didn't think we'd be getting much farther today.

I sat down but left space between the two of us. I wanted an explanation, not temptation.

As if looking at his body wasn't temptation enough.

"What are you, then?" I'd met a Detyen who had nothing to do with Ryklin before, and he'd seemed perfectly normal. Of course, he'd turned out to be a crazy murderer, so maybe the stoic thing was preferable.

Ryklin was contemplative, choosing his words carefully before he spoke. "This is not something you can speak of to anyone else. It goes beyond secret. My people kill to keep anyone from knowing."

I glanced around, back towards the river and then out at the trees. "Who am I going to tell?" In that moment, it felt like we were never going to make it to the mine. Or, if we did, then there was no way we'd be able to contact our friends.

"It had to be said," was his reply.

I nodded. My lips were sealed.

"What do you know about Detyens?" he asked. "Do you know about the Denya Price?"

"What's a denya?" Even with his monotone,

there was a note of reverence there. It had to be important. "Is that like a god or something?"

"It is the Detyen word for mate," he explained.

Mate. The word echoed in my head, bouncing around from synapse to synapse and reverberating through me. Goosebumps rose on my arms, and I tried to tell myself it was the cool air.

Yeah. Lying to myself never worked.

"A hundred years ago, our home planet, Detya, was destroyed. I am descended from some of the survivors. I was raised in the Detyen Legion and lived among them until nearly five years ago." He paused, but I didn't interrupt. I sensed there was a lot more to his story. "The Denya Price is a genetic quirk. A curse, some might say. If we do not find mates by the time we reach the age of thirty, we die."

I had to cover my mouth to keep a sound from escaping. That was horrible.

"But there is a way to avoid that, for those willing to pay an even higher price."

"A higher price than death?" I wanted to reach out and grab him, to shake him or hug him or comfort him. Or perhaps I was looking for comfort for myself.

"We are called the soulless," he said as if that was an answer.

Maybe it was, even if I still didn't know what it meant.

"Some of us in the Legion volunteer to undergo the procedure. It does something, though I'm not sure of the exact details. It tricks our bodies into circumventing the Deyna Price, but in doing so it also deadens our emotions. I have been soulless for about six years now. If I act like a robot, now you know why. All I have is logic."

That wasn't true. I almost said it out loud but managed to clamp my mouth shut. But it *wasn't*. If Ryklin was a being of pure logic, he would have never jumped into that escape pod to come after me. He wouldn't have even come to say goodbye.

"Drex was like you," I realized. Pippa's boyfriend —her mate? —had seemed cold at first, though I hadn't spent much time around him. Now he was as doting as a woman could dream of.

"Drex is nothing like me," he snapped.

Right. Not a single emotion to be found there.

"If the Legion is so keen to keep you secret, why are you here? Or, well, up there," I shot my gaze up towards the sky, as if Nebula Outpost might be hovering right overhead.

"I was slated for execution for deviation. My commanding officer helped me escape instead." He said it as if it wasn't horrifying.

"What? Why? What did you do?" Nothing about Ryklin would make me call him deviant. And I *wasn't* letting my mind go down that path.

He shook his head absently. In someone who knew they had emotions I'd say it was disbelief. "I asked for R&R, just as regular soldiers are entitled to. And when it was denied, I made a report detailing exactly why the soulless should be entitled to down time. We don't need emotions to need rest."

"That sounds entirely reasonable. And they wanted to execute you for it?" If his commanding officers were here right now, they'd be getting a piece of my mind.

"There are ... risks ... that come with being soul-less. If one does not act as expected, it needs to be dealt with immediately." Even he didn't sound convinced.

"Well, I'm glad you're not dead." A cool breeze blew over the river, and I shivered. I got up and checked my clothes, but they were still wet and freezing to the touch. I wasn't putting them back on unless I had to.

At least my canteen and comm had survived my

plunge. Not that the comm was much use down here, and I'd need to let it dry out completely before I powered it up.

"Come sit close to me," Ryklin said. "It will be warmer."

"You want to cuddle for warmth?" The flirtatious words were out of my mouth before I could stop them, so I grinned and strutted toward him as if I meant it.

He watched me, gaze intent. He looked absolutely ravenous, and he didn't even know it.

I sat down next to him and leaned against his chest, skin to skin. He was an inferno, but as we touched, he flinched. "Is something wrong?" I asked. This wasn't the first time.

"It's nothing."

"Don't lie." I tried to pull away, but his arm tightened on me. Almost like he wanted me there.

But he wasn't supposed to want anything.

"I don't lie," he responded. And then, after a moment, he relented. "When I touch you, I have a reaction. Pain. I don't know why, but you need the warmth."

I pulled away harder this time, and he had to let me go if he didn't want to truly force me in place. "I'm *hurting* you? How? Why?" My gaze raked up and down his naked skin as if I could see some sort of mark. "Are you allergic to me or something?"

"It's fine," he insisted. "Perhaps some unknown reaction. I don't normally touch people. The pain is bearable, and you are cold. Sit down."

I should let myself suffer to prevent his pain, but I recognized the stubborn set of Ryklin's face. I'd seen a similar expression on my own face when I was determined to have my way. And with the sun getting low, it was getting colder. We'd have to get up and make camp soon.

I sat back down next to Ryklin, holding myself stiff, afraid to relax against him, but my body quickly gave up that fight. "Tell me if it gets worse," I said.

"I think it improves with time," he said. "It is already better."

"So, you really don't feel anything?" It was hard to believe, especially given what I'd seen from him so far.

"I do not," he confirmed.

"Then why have you been following me around?" I didn't mean to ask it. I shifted how I was sitting and unthinkingly put my hand down on Ryklin's beefy thigh.

He hissed.

I tried to snatch my hand away, but he covered it, holding it in place. "You may touch me," he said. "Perhaps it will make the pain dissipate."

I squeezed my hand against his muscles and watched his expression for any hint of an effect. He was as blank as ever. But for just half a blink I could have sworn there was something there in his eyes, that they'd shifted from their normal black in a flash of color, gone just as quickly.

His thigh was tense under my touch, and I stroked downward towards his knee. I wouldn't risk going any higher. Ryklin's breath was ragged, but his hand stayed on top of mine, as if he was convinced I might pull away at any moment.

As if he wanted me to keep touching him.

My own body was definitely heating up, and I would have gladly taken his palm just about anywhere he wanted to put it. But this wasn't sexual, at least I didn't think it was. He was only wearing a thin pair of underwear, and they wouldn't hide much of anything. Of course, I was keeping my gaze away from the danger zone.

No need for temptation.

I flipped my hand over and entwined our fingers together for a moment. This touch wasn't anything, but it affected me like I was under his spell. My body was tight with want, flushed and desperate for more. But if Ryklin noticed, he said nothing.

I disentangled our fingers and scraped my hand down his palm and over his wrist then up his forearm.

Ryklin's tongue darted out to lick his lips, and that just about broke my will.

Then dark green blood started to trickle out of his nose.

13

PIPPA

"He just left in the middle of the night?" Drex was sitting on our couch and reading the note Zyrus had sent him. Ryklin was gone without a trace, and the only evidence that he'd ever existed was his pissed off boss and the note he'd left.

A note he had *not* included Drex on.

Maybe I was a hypocrite to be angry about that, but Drex and Ryklin had been roommates for nearly five years. Surely that meant he should tell my mate something.

Drex set his communicator down, his expression serious. He was still getting used to feeling after so many years without, and his expressions were either so minute they were nearly impossible to read or so broad they seemed like a joke. "I think he was worried about his mental state."

"Worried?" Ryklin was as soulless as they came.

He gave me a look. "You know what I mean."

Yes, I did. The soulless didn't have emotion, true, but they operated in a language full of it, and sometimes there was no better way to say something than to use a word that wasn't exactly precise to their condition but conveyed the meaning. "Why do you think he was worried?"

"I saw him the other day, and it looked like he was about to throw himself out the airlock. We spoke briefly and parted. And then there's Noelle. Do you think she knows?"

"I haven't seen her." It wasn't strange, exactly. Sure, we were best friends and neighbors and worked for the same department, but days could go by without a word between us. And she was off working in Sector J, which was so far off that she wasn't bothering to stop in the changing room before or after her shift.

It wasn't weird. But with Ryklin gone, something felt off.

"Where are you going?" Drex asked as I slipped on my shoes.

"To ask Noelle." Obviously.

My mate didn't follow. He was probably exchanging messages with Zyrus to try and find out whatever he could about Ryklin. Drex wasn't soulless anymore, but he still felt responsible for his men.

One of the many loveable things about him.

I pounded on Noelle's door and tried not to think of a time two months ago when I'd pounded on another woman's door. Fran couldn't answer because she was dead, because a madman had been stalking the station and had murdered her in a desperate bid for his own survival.

Now he was rotting on a prison colony. It didn't feel like justice, but at least it was over.

Noelle didn't answer.

There was a trick to opening these doors as long as the mechanical lock wasn't engaged, and I was tempted to do it, something urging me to believe that something was wrong with Noelle. What if she was sick? What if she'd fallen in the shower and hit her head?

Drex joined me and covered my hand with his own when I tried to knock again. I'd probably knock until I was bloody if he didn't stop me. "She's clearly not in her room," he said.

"Then where is she?" It came out a little more ragged than I wanted.

He wrapped his arms around me and held me tight. "I'm sure she's fine. Send her a message. Invite her over for dinner. We'll tell her about Ryklin together. It will all be okay."

I wanted to believe that.

I sent the message and waited for a response. But I didn't get one.

And she didn't show up for dinner.

14

RYKLIN

The bleeding stopped after Noelle tore herself out of my grasp and stared at me, eyes wide and panicked. I wiped my hand across my face and looked at the blood. I had a headache, a pounding in my temples that had been steadily building with every moment that Noelle touched me. But I hadn't told her to stop.

I hadn't *wanted* her to stop.

I could see that she was desperate to ask questions, but I had no answers. My clothing was dry enough, so I pulled them back on and watched as she did the same. Something about seeing her naked skin made me want to reach out and touch, just as she'd touched me. But if receiving touch had caused my nose to bleed, I could only imagine what might happen if I gave.

I shouldn't want it at all. I was soulless.

I was fixated.

I had to be.

Whatever fixation was, I'd tripped over that final step and fallen fully into it. My entire being felt attuned to Noelle, and there was something wild within me battering against my discipline to get out.

We built a fire at the edge of the beach, on the rocks where we wouldn't have to worry about it spreading. It wouldn't make for comfortable sleeping, but it would be safe enough. And tomorrow we should find the mine.

And then I would need to let Noelle go.

No.

The denial tore out of me, and I had to breathe deep to keep from speaking the word aloud. Nebula Outpost was Noelle's home. She belonged there. I could find some other place to live, some other planet where I would be no danger to her.

But my body rebelled at the thought of leaving her.

I forced myself to leave her by the fire as I tried to hunt more rabbits, but there were none to be found. Strange, but perhaps there were larger predators in the area, something that made them run.

Or maybe they heard me coming.

I heard a high-pitched shriek and went running back towards the beach only to find a fish flopping around near the edge of the water and Noelle standing up to her ankles, shirt off once more, as she stared at the water as if she could make the fish jump out of it with the power of her mind.

The dying fish on the beach was evidence that maybe she had.

"It's so gross, they're all touching my feet!" She hopped a bit in the shallows then bent down and came up with another fish in her hands, but it squirmed out and made it safely back to the water. "Damn it!"

Before I could take my boots off to assist, she grabbed another fish and threw it at the shore before sprinting out of the water as if it might bite her. "There, we have dinner." She pointed at the large fish on the ground. "You can use your, uh," she made a fist and swiped down with her wrist, imitating claws, "to clean those, right?"

"I can." There was something light in my chest, and I had the strangest urge to do ... something.

Perhaps I was just hungry and satisfied that we would have dinner.

What else could it be?

As I worked on the fish, Noelle pulled her shirt back on and rested her legs near the fire to let the bottoms of her pants dry. "They were all swarming in the water," she said. "That's why I could catch them. I figured it wouldn't hurt to give it a shot."

I could have pointed out that she could have been swept away in the river a second time, but I didn't. She hadn't gone deep, and she was an intelligent woman. I trusted her.

As night fell around us, we ate our fish.

It had been a long day, and I was ready to sleep, but Noelle was sitting up and looking into the fire. "I wonder if we should tell ghost stories. That's what you're supposed to do when you camp."

"Do you know any?" Soldiers in the Legion had plenty of stories to share, sights seen throughout the galaxy, unbelievable tales of daring and triumph. But I didn't think I had any about ghosts.

Noelle sprang into a tale about a widowed woman and her six dead husbands, all drowned in different shipwrecks. For some, it might have been scary, but all I could hear was Noelle's voice, the way her tone rose and fell, wrapping around me like an embrace.

I wanted her to keep speaking and never stop. I wanted her to move closer to me and touch me again.

I just wanted.

I shouldn't be able to. This wasn't what I was. But what was obsession if not want? What was fixation?

Or was it something else?

Drex had acted erratically before he realized that Pippa was his denya. He'd made decisions I hadn't understood and had acted in ways that went against every rule we had to adhere to as soulless Detyens. But it was all because he'd found his mate, and his emotions had somehow reawakened.

Could that be what this was? Could Noelle be my denya?

The want was so strong it made my gut clench. If Noelle was my denya, wouldn't I know it? We recognized our mates on sight. That was how it always worked. And I'd been seeing her around the ship for years. I may have become fixated, but there was no bond.

Then again, Drex had not immediately recognized Pippa. Perhaps it had something to do with the procedure that made us soulless.

I wanted it too much to believe it could be true. But perhaps refusing to believe it in this case was the illogical path.

Thinking about it was only confusing me further.

"And then the sea goddess rose out of the sea with her six undead merman husbands and slew the banshee before she could send any men to a watery grave!" Noelle ended with a flourish. "Now it's your turn."

I stared at her, at the flickering firelight reflecting off her hair. Her face glowed with warmth, and her eyes were bright with the story. I was no storyteller; I was bound to disappoint. "I have no stories to tell."

She opened her mouth and then quickly closed it, giving me a considering look. "Then what do you want to do?"

Sleep, I should have said. Or corrected her that a soulless Detyen could want nothing. But in that moment, it wasn't true. "I want to touch you." It was a secret shared between us, down here where no one could catch me, where no one could see the devia-tion. There was no worry, no rules. It was anathema to the soulless, but I would have shooed rescuers away in that moment if it meant I could spend more time with her.

Did that make her my mate or just my obsession?

Noelle's expression turned serious, but she scooted closer until we were nearly touching, only a breath between us. But she didn't reach out. No, this was my desire, my job.

I could still feel the ghost of her hands on me, though any pain it had caused had faded.

I started with her hand, and there was the explosion of pain in the back of my skull. It was even worse than before, prickling all down my neck and into my spine, like a limb that had fallen asleep and was trying to wake.

But I kept touching and ignored the pain. I traced my fingers over her hand, memorizing every curve and callus. I hadn't noticed her hands before, but they were strong, just as strong as the rest of her, even if she was softer than me in places.

Her hand twitched under my touch, and Noelle watched me, expression rapt.

I didn't dare kiss her. But that forbidden desire was there.

I brought her hand up to my face, cradling it

against my cheek, and her breath caught. And the pain grew. It was fire under my skin now, but I didn't care. I wanted her touch, and if it hurt then I would bear it.

I pressed her palm against my face, and Noelle leaned closer, her eyes falling half closed, and her lips parted.

"Ryklin ...," she breathed my name, and it was like a prayer, like a promise.

I leaned in and captured her lips before she could say anything else.

There was a burst of pain, and then a rush of heat. I was kissing her, and my body was on fire with need. I opened my mouth, old instinct driving me, and Noelle moaned.

Something in me roared to life, and then an avalanche of pain washed over me, and everything went black.

15

NOELLE

RYKLIN WENT limp in the middle of the kiss.

On instinct, I wrapped my arms around him and gently guided him down before he could fall near the fire. My heart beat wildly, both from the kiss and from the fact that the guy who'd kissed me had just *passed out*.

What in all the hells?

"Ryklin, wake up." I ran my fingers down his cheek, flashing back to yesterday when he landed on Nebula. How was that only yesterday? It felt like a lifetime had passed since then, since everything had changed. "Come on."

He had a pulse, so that was good, and his nose wasn't bleeding. Was he going to wake up? Why was he unconscious?

Oh gods, what if he'd hit his head in the river and I hadn't noticed? I'd heard that head wounds could be tricky like that; that a person could be walking and talking one minute and go down the next.

I wanted to shake him, but if something was wrong with his brain, that would definitely make it worse.

Panic pulsed in my veins. If we were back on the ship, this would be okay. They had actual medical equipment there and professionals who knew what they were doing.

But people still died sometimes even with access to the best medbots and doctors we had.

I squeezed my eyes shut before I did something stupid like cry. Tears wouldn't help anyone at that moment.

Maybe I should splash water on his face? I'd seen that work in vids. But I didn't think adventure shows from far off planets were good guidelines for medical treatment.

How long had he been out? A minute? Two? Why wasn't he waking up?

Something snapped in the woods, and I froze. As far as I knew, there weren't any large animals on Nebula. Nothing should be making noises I could hear.

But woods had a sound of their own, I reasoned. Back home on Thanatos, sometimes the shadows seemed to whisper with minds of their own.

The whispers I was hearing now weren't the shadows. A second twig snapped, and then someone spoke, though the words were swallowed by the encroaching night around us.

There wasn't supposed to be anyone on Nebula. The place had been abandoned a decade ago after the explosion. But I was definitely hearing voices. Was there someone down there with us?

Or was there some hallucinogenic quality to the fish I'd eaten for dinner?

"Do you want to miss the shipment, idiot?" a man said. He was speaking Interstellar Common and sounded like the kind of guy that liked to hit things. Though the smack of flesh and "ow!" from his companion could have been my tip off there.

They had to be close. If they came out onto the beach, they might see the fire. Ryklin and I had set up in a natural alcove that protected us from some of the elements and possibly from sight, but we hadn't been thinking of hiding. What need was there on an abandoned planet?

Ryklin twitched and then groaned, and my relief

was short lived as I worried the sound might echo. I shoved my hand over his mouth and gave him a harsh shake of my head.

"Did you hear something?" one of the men asked.

"We wouldn't hear anything out here," said the other.

Ryklin covered my hand with his own and eased it off his mouth. He looked at me gravely as he sat and then stared towards the woods. The voices were starting to move away.

He stood. "Stay here," he whispered.

I stood up too. "Not a chance."

16

NOELLE

Night hadn't completely fallen. We wouldn't have been able to follow if it had. The two men weren't making any effort to hide their trail, but after a few minutes, their voices disappeared completely. I heard the sound of an engine firing up, and Ryklin took off running with me right behind him.

We made it to a spot farther down the beach just in time to see a small craft launch itself into the air and break for the sky.

We weren't the only ones on Nebula. At least, we hadn't been.

"What's going on?" I asked, as if Ryklin might have any more answers than I did.

"I don't know." Once the ship was high enough in the sky that there was no way they could spot us on the ground, he moved forward to examine the launch area.

There were three large, empty pallets sitting near an indentation in the mud that might have been from the ship's ramp. There was also a flashlight laying on the ground. I scooped it up and pressed the power button, letting out a whoop of joy when it shined bright. The sun had nearly set, and it was getting hard to see.

"Any ideas?" I wasn't a sleuth; I was a tech. I fixed things that were broken. I hated puzzles, and this had all the makings of something bad.

"Do you know why they never reopened the mine?" Ryklin asked. "Or why whatever company owns it never used the planet for anything else?"

"Something about contamination, maybe?" I'd asked the same question not long after arriving on Nebula Outpost and had been given a similarly vague answer.

"Then why keep the Outpost running?" He held out his hand, and I handed over the flashlight. He ran it over deep ruts in the ground that I realized came from wheels. I didn't see a vehicle, so either it had been driven away or the two men in the woods had taken it with them.

"What are you thinking?" I asked. I remembered

the drug dealers up on the station, the crime that seemed to get worse by the day. Nebula Outpost was no paradise, but it couldn't be that much worse than any other place. "They don't need a whole planet just to run drugs." Sure, there were incredibly expensive, exotic substances that were only produced in certain corners of the galaxy, but those drugs tended to stay there. You couldn't charge enough to move Lux or Benit in quantity. Small shipments came from specialty couriers and only for the insanely rich.

Solar Flare and other drugs like it could be made anywhere. No need for an empty planet or complex shipping.

"Not drugs." Ryklin followed the tracks for a few steps before stopping and flashing his light into the dark woods. "This could be a way station for smugglers, a convenient place to repair without taxes or questions. Or perhaps there's some illegal mining going on. We won't know if we stay here." The beam from his flashlight still shone into the darkness, telling me exactly where he wanted to go.

"Seems like it might not be wise to follow in the dark with no backup." I strained to hear any hint that the two in the ship had friends, but there were only the sounds of wildlife and the breeze in the trees.

"It also wouldn't be wise to wait on the beach if we're so near their launch path. They might have seen our fire." His voice was as steady as ever, but I could have sworn I heard a hint of a dare in it.

Emotionless, my ass.

I wavered for only a moment before gesturing for him to lead on. We had no one to report this to, and no help was coming. If some shady figures had taken over the mine, we'd never be able to use it to get a message back to Nebula Outpost. And, hey, maybe there'd be an extra ship waiting for us. If we were really lucky, we'd be home in a matter of hours.

Nothing about the last two days told me we were lucky.

The trail cut a path through the forest, and there was no attempt at covering the tracks. Whoever was working here was confident they wouldn't be discovered. Or that they could handle anyone who crossed their path.

"Are you feeling alright?" I asked Ryklin after a few minutes of walking. I'd been keeping my eye on him, and not just because he was the only light in the forest. There was no hint that he'd passed out, nothing to give away that I'd worried he might die less than an hour ago.

"Yes, I'm functional," he said.

So, we were back to that.

I wasn't letting it stand. "We kissed, and you passed out. What was that all about?" My voice got a bit louder than intended, and I had to claw it back.

"I don't know. It should not happen again." Robot. He was back to being Mr. Robot, acting like there was nothing between us and he was all neurons and programming.

I didn't buy it for a second.

And he said *should* not.

Not could not.

That was an opening.

"So, you don't want to kiss me again?" I asked. I wanted his lips on mine again desperately, even as I dreaded it. What if he had an even stronger reaction? Could my kiss kill him?

Maybe we really shouldn't kiss again.

"I cannot want anything," he reminded me. Even tone, unbothered. I hated it.

"I think you're lying to me." This wasn't the time or place to be having this conversation. I knew that. There could be bad guys at the end of this trail, and Ryklin was the only one with any chance of winning a fight. But I feared that if I let it go for the night, he'd never let me bring it up again. There was something intimate about the darkness, something that allowed secrets to slip out.

I wanted all his secrets.

"The soulless do not lie," he said.

Lying.

I took two long steps and grabbed his wrist, forcing him to stop walking. "Talk to me, Ryklin, tell me what's really going on."

He looked down at me, and his nostrils flared. I couldn't say for sure with the flashlight pointed the other way, but I thought he was looking at my lips. We definitely couldn't kiss here, not if he might pass out again.

But my tongue darted out anyway, lips suddenly dry. I wanted to taste him again. And I wanted him awake for the whole thing. "Why did you pass out?" I asked again. It felt like the key to this whole thing, as if this was some solvable puzzle. And even if I hated puzzles, I had a pressing need to solve this one.

He'd told me he was soulless, that he felt nothing. I knew that meant there could be nothing between us. I'd never *wanted* anything between us.

And now it was all I could imagine. It was in my grasp, if only I could figure this out.

He said he was nothing like Drex, but I had to wonder if that was true. I wished I could talk to Pippa. Maybe she would have the answers I needed. And it would also mean we weren't stuck on a not-so-abandoned planet and possibly in danger from smugglers.

He opened his mouth to answer, but then his head snapped to the side, and he twirled away, standing in front of me, the claws on one hand out while his other hand clutched the flashlight.

Then the first stone came flying our way.

17
RYKLIN

I TACKLED Noelle to the ground, covering her with my body and prepared to absorb any fire that came our way. Stones hailed down on my back, but most of them were too small to even bruise.

Why weren't they using weapons?

The hail stopped after a moment, and Noelle squirmed out of my hold. It had an unexpected effect on my body, sending an entirely different kind of heat straight to my groin. I had to curl my hands into fists to keep from reacting farther. It was another impossibility. The soulless didn't lust.

But she aroused feelings in me I couldn't deny.

I just didn't understand them. And that was dangerous.

"Do you think it's a trick?" Noelle whispered, her lips ghosting against my ear, nearly enough to make me shiver.

"I don't know." And all the not knowing that Nebula kept throwing at us was untenable. I thought I heard someone coming our way, the branches and leaves snapping as they scored their path through the dark woods. "I'll distract them. I want you to run."

She stiffened and curled her fingers into my arm. "Absolutely not. I'm not leaving you here." Her voice was fierce. "Besides, I can barely see a thing. I'll get lost in a second."

Even the flashlight would do no good. It would be a beacon to anyone looking for her.

My stomach roiled and churned as certainty that all was lost rolled over me. Was this what despair felt like? Some emotions were better left behind.

I stood, careful to keep myself between our attackers and Noelle. I would protect her until my final breath, no matter how soon that moment came. If this was our end, at least I could give her the comfort of knowing someone had fought for her.

It would not be enough.

"We mean you no harm," came a gruff voice, still

swallowed by darkness. "You don't hurt us, we don't hurt you."

The air seemed to stand still with expectation. I peered into the darkness where the voice had come from but could see nothing. Then there was the snap of a twig from the path behind us, and I spun around just as three people holding a makeshift flashlight and crudely fashioned spears stepped onto the path.

My mind analyzed the threat even as it spun in confusion.

Human.

Thirties, perhaps.

Gaunt but not starving.

No projectiles.

Standing too close to Noelle.

I was rougher than I should have been as I surged in front of her, but she would have to forgive me later. These people may not have had blasters, but a spear could be just as deadly. And from the way the man on the right was gripping his, he'd wielded it before.

"Are you with *them*?" the twitchy man asked.

There was a woman in the center of the group. She was my age or a bit younger, mid-thirties, with dark, braided hair and a wicked scar on her face. She shot the man who'd spoken a look I couldn't interpret. "If they were, we'd be dead." Then she turned back to Noelle and me. "Follow us." There was no other option.

Noelle took my hand, and that familiar pain shot up my arm. But she squeezed my hand, and without looking at her I knew what it meant. She wanted to see where these people would take us.

Me too.

A fourth man was waiting on the other edge of the clearing. He'd been the distraction to allow the other three to flank us. They'd done this before. And whoever we'd seen earlier was likely the threat the twitchy man was referring to. Unless Nebula was hiding even more from us.

The twitchy man and the gruff man took the rear while the two women in the group were in front. Noelle and I may have been able to make a run for it, but I couldn't risk them catching one of us. If they took her, I'd come to get her back. If they took me, she'd surrender herself for my safety.

We weren't tied up, and these humans hadn't done much harm to us yet. I didn't consider some flung rocks a massive assault. That had been a test to see if we had the capability of firing back.

I smelled smoke before I saw the light of it. And I didn't see any hint of the encampment until we passed a dense outcropping of trees and climbed over a small hill. And then it was suddenly there, nestled in the bottom of a valley, a collection of clobbered together shacks and tents that I guessed could house a hundred or so people.

We passed by sentries as we made our way down the hill, and from the very careful path we took, I assumed there might be booby traps waiting for anyone who strayed from safety.

"What is this place?" Noelle asked, voice full of confusion and a little wonder.

Strange that I could hear that so easily. Other people's emotions were often as elusive to the soulless as our own. Perhaps I just knew Noelle well enough now for that not to be the case.

I was lying to myself.

The woman who'd spoken before answered. "Home, or what's left of it." She didn't elaborate.

This place wasn't some quickly put together camp. It was ramshackle, but lived in. These people had been here for some time. I wondered if it was ten years. The mining company said no one survived the explosion.

Had they lied?

Another group of armed humans met us at the bottom of the hill. "These aren't our usual friends, Astrid," said the middle-aged man leading the second group of spear bearers.

Astrid, the leader and speaker in our group, looked us over. "We found them near a launch site, Davis. They didn't fire back. And he's not Oscavian." She gave me a look, clearly waiting for me to supply my species.

"Detyen," I said.

Astrid shook her head. "Can't say I've heard much about Detyens. Do you have a name?"

"Ryklin." I had no reason to withhold it.

"And what about her?" She nodded towards Noelle.

"She speaks for herself," Noelle didn't surprise me by saying. "And her name's Noelle. Human, if that wasn't clear."

I spotted a dozen or so people in this tiny village, and they were all human, but I didn't know if that was indicative that the entire village was human or that the non-humans were off doing something else.

"You take him," she told Davis. "We'll take the girl. I want answers."

"What? No!" Noelle struggled as two men came forward to grab her.

I spun around, a sound of impossible fury coming out of my mouth as I bared my teeth and claws. I pushed the men away and grabbed Noelle close, refusing to let anyone near her.

No one touched my mate.

18

RYKLIN

Denya.

The certainty settled over me as the humans got into formation, their spears pointed straight for me. They'd run me through in an instant, but I could take out at least one of them, maybe two. I could make them pay for what they wanted to do to us.

Denya.

I heard it with every beat of my heart, the realization sinking deep into the soul that should have been dead and long gone. Anger. That was a feeling. Fear was there as well.

Regret.

And the driving need to claim my mate. It pounded within me, and if we hadn't been surrounded by ten armed humans with grim expressions on their faces, Noelle would have been in my arms right that moment.

Astrid held up a fist, and the humans retracted their spears. "Fine, we'll talk to you together. Does that satisfy you, Mr. Ryklin?" Her voice was calm, as if that might steady my own emotions.

"My clan name is NaHavoc." I didn't move from where I stood, but I let my claws retract.

My mate put her hand over my arm and stepped out from behind me. "There's no need for violence," she said. She was speaking to me as much as them. But she was touching me.

It hurt, still, but the hurt was nothing compared to the need even that slight press of her fingers brought forward. I breathed deep, both to calm myself and trying to pull in her scent.

All I could smell was the fire and some sort of roasting meat.

Astrid and Davis led us toward that fire and sat us down at a crudely constructed table. Two men left and came back after a moment with plates laden with food and cups full of water. Noelle didn't hesitate to eat or drink, and though I was wary, I followed her lead. If these people wanted to kill us, they'd use their spears. There was no need for poison.

Once we'd finished, the same men took our plates and cups away.

We weren't tied up. We were out in the open. It still felt a bit like we were prisoners.

I took my mate's hand in my own and didn't miss the way Astrid's eyebrows rose at the gesture. Our hands rested on the table, a clear sign we had no weapons. I didn't want them to think I was a threat.

"What is this place?" Noelle asked. "How are you here? Nebula is supposed to be abandoned."

Davis snorted at that. Astrid gave us a wry look. "Yeah, that's what the bosses said." She pointed to the scar on her face. "I got this in the explosion. It was right at the shift change, but I'd slept through my alarm and was running late. I was sure they'd dock my pay or have me on shit duty for a month for it. I was just about to enter one of the outbuildings when I heard the first explosion. Everyone inside died. And then no one came to rescue us."

Noelle's fingers squeezed mine. "They just left you here?" Her voice was horrified.

"They did," said Davis. He and Astrid were both circumspect. They'd had a decade to process the horror. "No matter how many times we called for help, no one came. We stopped calling, eventually. How do you know about Nebula?"

My mate pointed towards the sky. "We live on Nebula Outpost." Then she sucked in a shuddering breath. "Do you know the Vales? My friend Pippa's parents were miners. Did they—"

Astrid shook her head before Noelle could finish her question. "No one named Vale lives in the village. I'm sorry."

"Oh."

Hope could be cruel, even when it was so short lived.

"So, there's still a whole space station hovering above this planet, and no one could bother to send help for, what's it been, nine years?" Davis was scowling.

"Ten," said Noelle. "It's been just under ten years."

Astrid closed her eyes for a moment, taking that in. Then her expression was all business once more. "Why are you here? How?"

"We were in escape pods that crashed. We ejected by accident."

There was no need to go into the whole story, but Noelle launched into it anyway, and Astrid and Davis listened with steely expressions.

"Then we heard those two guys," she said. "We were camping on the side of the river and heard them. We followed, but they made it to their craft before we could catch up. Any idea what that's about?"

"Smugglers," Davis spat. "They've got an illegal mining operation going on in the wreckage of the old mine. They dig around our old friends' corpses to extract whatever they can. They bring in slaves from wherever you get them in this part of the galaxy. A few have escaped, and we've taken them in. Most die within a few months. It's toxic down there, and they don't provide safety equipment. We're far enough away that they haven't found our village yet, though I don't like how close they were today."

"They were probably stealing a bit for themselves," Astrid suggested. "No reason to hide a ship this far out otherwise."

"So, they don't know you're here?" I asked.

Astrid laughed mirthlessly. "Oh, they know. They've stolen just as many from us as we've saved. But they don't know where we live. Something about the natural formation of this area makes it hard to scan from the air, and we've got sentries all around to make sure no one gets too close. It's not safe, exactly, but it's as safe as we can make it."

"And you've never been able to get a message out?" Noelle asked.

"We haven't tried in years, not since the smugglers moved in," said Astrid. "Too risky. After the first few months, we started to think something might have been interfering with the signal."

"Yeah, the assholes who blew us up for insurance money," muttered Davis.

"You think it was on purpose?" Noelle leaned forward, eyes wide.

"On purpose or not, someone made a choice not to look for survivors," said Astrid, shooting Davis a warning look. "It's getting late, and you must be tired, given all you've been through. Let us provide you with a place to stay. We can speak more in the morning."

"And if we wish to go?" I didn't trust these survivors, even if they'd fed us. They were doubtlessly hiding things, and I wasn't sure their story added up.

"Ryklin ...," Noelle said in warning.

But Astrid kept her eyes on me. "Stay the night," she said, the slightest hint of a threat under her words. "We wouldn't want you getting lost in the woods."

19
NOELLE

THE SHACK we were led to was better than sleeping on the cold ground with no blankets for another night. But before going through the door, I tipped my head up and looked at the starry sky. Nebula Outpost was up there somewhere, too high and too small to be seen by my eyes.

Did they realize we were gone yet? Was someone looking for us?

The existence of this settlement suggested help may not be coming.

Astrid took a pack from the man walking with us and handed it over. "Here are some clothes. There's a tub in there if you want to clean your own and a bit of soap. There should be a rainwater collector out back for your water. There's an outhouse out there too."

With that, she left us.

The shack wasn't much. A single room with a fireplace, the tub she mentioned, and a bed fashioned from blankets—no mattress. And no bathroom. Right. Outhouse. No indoor plumbing or any other amenities. But the roof was nice.

Ryklin was staring at me.

I could feel his gaze on my back as I pulled out the clothes that Astrid had given us. They were old, probably scavenged from the miners' housing before they all left to make this camp.

The tub was tiny and made of metal. Ryklin wouldn't fit in it, and it would be tight if I tried. But at least we could clean our clothes. "Do you think you could fill this?" I asked, offering the pitcher hanging off the side of the tub.

Ryklin took it, and our hands brushed.

I shivered.

Something was different.

I didn't let myself think about it as I quickly stripped out of my clothes and changed into the clean ones. I tossed my dirty laundry in the tub and thanked Ryklin when he came back with the water. I took the pitcher from him so that he could change in private and filled it from the water out back.

The soap wasn't like anything I'd ever used on the station, crude and somehow made from whatever supplies they had down here. It felt fatty in my hands and didn't foam up, but since the water was turning dark with grime, I figured it was doing its job. Ryklin took the tub and dumped it out before wringing the clothes out and hanging them up.

It was the most exhausting version of laundry I'd ever done. Up on Nebula Outpost, I put my clothes in the hamper, and they were whisked away, returned a day or two later, clean as if by magic.

I missed home.

I sat down on the bed area and pulled my legs in close. "What do you think of all this?" I asked. I'd been certain we were dead when these people found us, and my brain was still trying to catch up to the fact that we were safe ... ish.

He lowered himself down beside me and took my hand. His face was still as neutral as ever, but there was something in his eyes, something almost like worry. "I don't want to lose you," he said.

My breath caught. That didn't sound like the allegedly emotionless man he claimed to be. And before I could respond, Ryklin leaned in and kissed me.

This wasn't like before. It wasn't a gentle exploration so quickly cut off. Now he kissed me like I was the air he breathed. His lips caressed mine, and then his tongue slid against the seam of my lips. I was eager to taste him and moaned into his embrace, my hands going up to his shoulders and grasping as if he might disappear at any moment.

I should have asked why he was kissing me, why things were different now. Instead, I clung to him with everything I had and fell back onto the blanket, bringing him with me. His heavy body settled over mine, and it felt like it was the only thing anchoring me to this planet.

Ryklin was my one constant in this unwanted adventure, and I didn't want to let him go. He pressed kisses down my neck as his hands began to explore my body. One of them dipped under the hem of my shirt, and a tingling thrill raced through me when he encountered bare skin.

He let out a rough breath, and I didn't know if that pain that assailed him before was threatening now. And the more he explored, the harder it was to think to ask.

His fingers were rough with callouses, but his

touch was deft as he gently cupped my breast, as if testing the weight of it.

"Ryklin ..." His name was a prayer on my lips.

He buried his head in my hair and murmured something I didn't quite hear.

"What?" I asked.

He didn't raise his head, just curled his hand tighter around me. "Mine."

My body went up in flames as need washed over me. It wasn't just enough to kiss, to touch. I needed everything he could give me and then some.

I'd never wanted to be claimed by any man, but one word from him tilted my entire world on its axis.

"Yes," I breathed.

He finally raised his head and stared down at me with glowing red eyes, something that might have looked demonic if I didn't trust him with everything I was. The light flickered for a moment before he blinked, and they returned to normal. "I want you now," he said, the words coming out like a groan.

"Please." It was as desperate as he sounded, though I managed to keep it mostly in a whisper. The walls of this shack were thin, and I didn't want anyone listening in.

But then he kissed me again, and I forgot everything else existed.

He released his hold on me only long enough to take off my shirt. I lifted my hips to help him drag my pants down and was about to help him get out of his borrowed clothes when he disrobed with disappointing efficiency.

But him naked was a sight to behold.

The only thing lighting the room was the fire, flickering yellow casting deep shadows on his teal skin. He was utterly alien and absolutely beautiful.

And I wanted him like nothing else.

"Let me see you, mate," he said, and I couldn't imagine denying him anything. And I was too far gone in that moment to realize what he was saying then.

I couldn't care.

I laid back and raised my arms over my head like some kind of ancient offering, something from back in the time of brutality and human sacrifice. He was the dark god come to claim me.

He bent over me, a hungry expression on his face, but all he did was look, eyes roving over me until I thought I might die from wanting. And then he did the unexpected and put his lips on the delicate skin of my wrist. My breath stuttered at the kiss, but my lungs failed me completely when he started trailing those lips upward.

He kissed up my arm, across the curve of my breast, and down my side, until he was on his knees between my spread legs. "Perfection." And then he licked my core, and I nearly levitated off the floor.

He put his hands on my hips to hold me down as he tortured me. He devoured my sex like a dying man consumed his first meal, and I couldn't control the sounds he dragged from me. I didn't want to. Especially not when I heard his groan of satisfaction.

The vibrations from it traveled up my spine, and I arched my back as my body seized, the pleasure that had been building from the first brush of his lips reaching a crescendo that left me unable to do anything but shudder.

It was the most incredible moment of my life.

But Ryklin didn't stop. If anything, he became more determined as he held me captive against his lips. Pleasure rolled over me in waves, and I didn't know how long it lasted, but I was drowning in it, and there was nowhere in the universe I'd rather be.

I clutched at his shoulders, desperate for something to anchor me to reality. I had no doubt that I'd fly apart if not for him.

He nipped at my clit, and stars danced before my eyes. And when he licked at me again, he didn't stop, tracing the opening of my sex and fucking me with his tongue.

The moment his lips brushed my center again, I broke.

Pleasure roared through me with enough power to rip me to shreds. And again, it was too much. Too much and not nearly enough. "I need you," I told him, my voice wrecked and throat sore, like I'd been screaming, even though my lips hurt from how hard I'd been biting them to keep quiet.

He gave me a final kiss and crawled back over my body, covering me with his heat. "Mine," he told me again, and I loved the way his voice sounded, guttural and filled with promise.

I didn't know what had come over him, but I wasn't complaining. Not about this. And not as I wrapped my hand around the impossibly hard cock that rested heavy against my thigh. "Ryklin," I whispered as he threw his head back and groaned.

"Yours," he said when he opened his eyes again. He grabbed my wrists and pinned them down, letting his body rest against mine. I could feel every inch of him, every ridge and line, every hot, silky bit of skin. He rolled his hips, and his erection rubbed against my core. "My mate."

Again, those words sent a wave of heat through me, pooling where his flesh pressed against my own.

I wanted to reach for him, but he didn't let me go. He lined up his cock with my center and pressed forward, entering me with excruciating slowness. He stretched me open as he entered, and I panted, not entirely sure how he could fit inside. He was built a bit differently than a human, his cock covered in intense ridges and veins that made me shiver as I felt every inch enter me.

It seemed impossible that he could go any deeper.

And yet he did.

I bit my lip when he bottomed out, so full of him that it seemed my body could only exist with his inside. He pressed kisses to my face, releasing my wrists and using his elbows to support himself so that he didn't crush me with his full weight. "Perfect, my mate is perfect."

I ran my fingers through his hair, which was surprisingly soft and silky despite its stiffness. "Make love to me." I didn't know what I was asking, but I wanted to belong to him with everything in me. I needed it like I needed air.

He drew his hips back slowly, and I clutched at his back, already afraid this might end too soon.

Then he thrust back in.

I saw stars again as pleasure consumed me. All I could do was hang on as Ryklin set a steady pace, claiming me again and again as he thrust in and out.

I wanted to live in this moment forever.

He trailed kisses over my cheek, jaw, and throat, murmuring what I assumed were Detyen words against my skin. And though I couldn't understand it, I understood the tone. It was full of reverence and affection and worship, and the way his body worshipped mine sent shivers up my spine.

It wasn't long before I was clutching at him as orgasm rose to consume me. My toes curled, and I opened my mouth in a silent scream as the pressure broke free and rushed out of me, sweeping away all thought.

He thrust one final time, emptying into me, and I swore I could feel something snapping into place in my chest, some missing piece I'd never known I needed finally there.

I smiled at Ryklin, but his eyes flashed red once more, then his mouth opened in horror, and he passed out.

20
NOELLE

My heartbeat started to calm a bit when Ryklin groaned and shifted, as if he were merely sleeping. I was getting used to this bad Detyen habit of passing out at inopportune moments, and we needed to get to the bottom of this if we were going to do that again.

And I definitely wanted to do that again.

My body still hummed with pleasure even as the vestiges of fear tried to take hold.

There was something wrong with my mate, and I needed him fixed.

Mate.

Me and Ryklin.

Hells. What was I supposed to do with that? If it had been someone else, I might have dismissed those words as the passion that came from sex, but not him. If I hadn't been so caught in the moment I might have realized it. Everything happening between the two of us suggested something special, something huge.

But would he still be mine when he woke up?

I was braced for rejection. Not the kind that came from some jerk getting what he wanted and discarding his partner, but the worse kind, the kind that went soul deep and told you the universe was against you.

I was ready to fight for Ryklin. Would he fight for us?

His eyes opened, and he groaned, curling in on himself as if he'd been punched. He was still gorgeous, all that naked skin on display just for me. My hands ached to touch, but I held myself back. We needed to have this conversation, and touching basically guaranteed it wouldn't happen. I probably should have put some clothes back on, but when Ryklin looked at me, his eyes going red and his nostrils flaring, I didn't regret my nakedness.

"Noelle," he rasped. He didn't say anything else.

That meant I had to do the talking. Fine. "I don't like it when you pass out like that."

He reached for me, and I surrendered against his

embrace. "Nor do I." There was more depth to his voice, layers I hadn't heard before, no longer the monotone he'd spoken in for all the time I knew him.

His lips trailed down my neck, soft enough that I shivered.

"We're talking right now," I said, though my words were more breathy than anticipated.

"We can talk later." His hand splayed out over my stomach and started to move downward.

I moaned into the touch but forced myself to cover his hand and stop its progress. "Talk first," I insisted. Even I could hear the complaint in my voice.

Ryklin let go. "Very well."

"You called me your mate." It was the word echoing around my mind. In the midst of our love-making, I didn't think too hard about it, but with the clarity that came afterward, all I could do was wonder if it was true. And there was only one person who could tell me that. "You said you didn't have a mate, that you couldn't. What's going on?" I wasn't accusing him of lying, not quite, but I had to know.

He heaved out a deep breath. "You remember that I told you that I'm nothing like Drex?"

"Yes."

"I appear to have been mistaken." He took my hand and laced our fingers together. "It no longer hurts to touch you."

A sense of relief washed over me. That was one less thing to worry about. "And the rest of the explanation?" My emotions were all tangled up. Joy, relief, fear, even a little anger. I didn't think Ryklin had lied to me, at least not intentionally, but the doubt was still there, too strong to be completely ignored.

"I only recognized you as my denya when they tried to part us as we entered the village." He raised our joined hands and kissed my fingers. "There wasn't a moment to tell you until we were alone. And then ..."

And then, indeed.

"How is this possible?" My heart had broken when he explained what it meant to be soulless, as if I'd known that he was the missing piece of me.

"I don't know." His arm tightened on me. "But some part of me must have recognized you from the beginning. It was why I couldn't stay away."

"The stalking." I'd been so angry about that, at least a little because part of me had come to anticipate the meetings, to want them. That forbidden want was nothing like the inferno raging in me now.

"I am sorry for causing you discomfort."

I smiled. "Is that what it was?"

He spun me around so that we were face to face. His expression was grave, but there was no hint of the emotionless man he'd once claimed to be. "You are my denya, Noelle."

A sense of rightness settled in me. But there was also worry. We were going to make it home, I was determined. I didn't want to live out the rest of my life in a shack on a mostly abandoned planet, even if I'd have Ryklin at my side. But would he still be this caring, dedicated man when we were up there, when there were expectations on who'd he'd been and who he was supposed to be?

I kissed him and let him pull me down to our pallet and put the worries aside until morning.

21

RYKLIN

THE WORLD around me was bright. My slightly damp shirt irritated my skin. And I was happy.

It was a strange sensation, a lightness in my chest that made me want to reach for my mate and kiss her breathless. There was also lingering doubt and worry for what might have happened if she hadn't accepted our bond.

It should have been irrelevant, but my mind had latched onto it.

Emotions were annoying.

And wonderful.

I took my mate's hand as we followed our noses to the smell of breakfast. There was a large brick stove set up in the center of the encampment, and several residents were working in practiced unison to put food on plates.

"We work in shifts." Astrid came up beside us as we joined the line. "I'm not such an early riser, so I usually take lunch or dinner. We're lucky that Nebula is so full of life. Finding food has never been an issue."

"Did you scavenge the bricks from the mine?" Noelle asked. "And how did you make the soap?"

"The thing they never tell you about survival is that it's all crafting after awhile." Astrid smiled and shook her head slightly. "Soap's not too hard to make, though luckily we have a few people who knew how. And we made the bricks too. Our quarters back at the mine were all wood and steel. We're working on cloth, but luckily the quartermaster's stores were mostly unharmed in the blast. There were supplies for nearly a thousand miners, so we can care for our clothes and use our stocks to resupply as needed."

An infant's wail cut through her talk. "There are children here?" I asked.

"Some. Most of us had birth control implants, but those fail after awhile." She looked up at the sky. "These kids shouldn't have to grow up like this."

"We're going to get back to Nebula Outpost," my

mate said with utter determination. "And we'll tell them about you. If you want off this planet, we'll get you."

Astrid didn't look convinced.

We'd barely sat at a table and started to eat when I noticed a sense of unease start to suffuse the crowd. I didn't stop eating, though Noelle barely touched her food.

A skinny man ran up to Astrid and whispered something in her ear. She cursed and stood. "I'm sorry, I need to go."

My mate watched her leave. "Is something wrong?"

"I think so."

She looked at her plate and tried to push it away. I placed my hand on the edge to keep it in place. "I'm not hungry."

"If things are about to go wrong, we don't know when we'll have our next meal. Eat what you can." It was experience learned from years in the Detyen Legion.

She glared at her plate for a moment but picked up the slice of flatbread and took a bite.

Several minutes later, Astrid came back, and villagers gathered around her, Noelle and I included. Whatever was going on, I wanted to know.

Wasn't curiosity strange?

"Rook and Solara are missing," she announced. There was an outbreak of murmurs, but her voice still carried on top of them. "Has anyone seen them since dawn?"

No one responded until ... "Maybe they snuck off together!" That voice was met with recrimination.

"Rook would never cheat on his husband! And Solara wouldn't try anything; she's a good woman." There was debate back and forth, but nothing of substance.

"I heard something drive by the edge of my patrol this morning," another voice cut through the crowd, and the rest quieted. "Just after dawn. Rook and Solara would have been gathering food near there. Could have been taken."

Astrid cursed. "Another of the gatherers heard screams. Was this on the western edge?" she asked the man.

"Yes."

"We need a headcount. Everyone report to your census leader. You know the drill." The group scattered, and Astrid turned to stride off.

Noelle and I went right after her. The human didn't get far. "Astrid—" Noelle tried to talk.

"It's not the time," Astrid cut her off. "We're

going to have to search the western edge in case Rook and Solara are injured. But chances are, some of those damned smugglers grabbed them. Either we'll find bodies, or they've been taken to work the mines. This isn't the first time this has happened."

"And if they've been taken?" She already sounded defeated.

Her expression turned even darker. "I have one hundred and thirty-seven other people to keep safe. I can't round up a force of our strongest fighters to storm the mine. They'll be killed. We'll see if we can find bodies, and maybe a small scouting group will try and follow the trail of the vehicle Cory heard. But if they're already in the mine, I can't help them."

"I want to be in that scouting group."

"Ryklin." Noelle's hand squeezed mine. A warning.

Astrid didn't immediately agree. "We'll discuss it later. Just stay put, either here or in your quarters. We can't afford to lose anyone else today."

22

NOELLE

THE ENTIRE ENCAMPMENT had sprung into motion, but Ryklin and I were the two pieces that didn't fit. We had nothing to do, and as that became more and more clear, we headed back to our shack. At the very least, we could stay out of the way.

Hours ticked by, or at least it felt like it. There were no clocks to be found, but the sun climbed steadily overhead. It heated the inside of the room until I ended up sitting outside just for a bit of breeze. Ryklin joined me.

"I need to go with that search party," he said, voice full of determination.

It filled my heart to hear that emotion, to know that I had put it there. But it made me sick to think of what he was saying. "These smugglers kill and enslave people. You can't risk that."

"We've been heading for the mine this whole time. That's where the comms equipment is. I can get a message out. Maybe someone will get off their ass and send these smugglers scattering. They're not used to a fight, especially not one coming from the sky." He sounded so reasonable, and maybe I would have agreed if he wasn't my mate. But I'd just given my heart to this man. I didn't want to lose him so soon.

"And if no one comes? No one's answered these people's calls for help in a decade."

"If I can get a message to my men, to Drex, they will come."

I hated to bring it up, but it had to be said. "Aren't your men soulless? They might write you off as a loss. No need to risk their lives to rescue you."

"Perhaps," he conceded, "but not Drex. And Drex will get them to move. We were all soldiers once. They'll come to help. And I've faced worse enemies than this. I'll come back to you. I promise."

I threw myself into his arms and squeezed my eyes shut so the tears wouldn't come. No way was I going to cry right now. "Fine. Then let's go find Astrid before they leave without you."

The heart of the encampment wasn't very busy. Whatever the people had to do, they were doing it elsewhere. A group of men and women—some human, some not—were suiting up, and Ryklin went to join them.

Astrid came to stand by me. "I didn't think you'd let him go."

"I don't want to." I could admit it to her. It had taken everything in me not to get on my knees and beg him to stay.

"If you want comms, it's right to send him. These assholes are careful. None of them carry anything strong enough to send a message off planet; they keep that all in their camp. My people will escort him as far as they can, but the priority is finding Solara and Rook. They'll cover him like he's one of their own." She didn't promise me that he'd make it back.

"His friends on the ship are former soldiers. If he can get a message out, they'll come. There's plenty of room on Nebula Outpost for everyone down here. If you want."

"Do you think we enjoy living like this?" She didn't sound mad, not exactly, but there was definitely something there. "We ran out of chocolate nine years ago. I haven't had coffee since the morning of the explosion. I only had three episodes left in this media show I was watching. And, well, the men here are nice enough, but it gets messy so quick and none of them are ... right." Her voice trailed off like she was thinking of something else.

"Right?" I prompted.

"Your man, I've seen his kind before. A very long time ago."

"He's Detyen. There aren't many of his kind left." Though I wasn't about to go into the whys.

"Detyen ..." A wistful smile pulled at the corner of her lips. "Do you ever wonder how your life might have been different if you said yes instead of nothing?"

"Doesn't everyone?" Ryklin and the others were walking away now, and I had to force my gaze away. I wasn't going to do something foolish like run after him. He knew what he was doing.

"Those are happier thoughts than anything else I have to deal with today. Come with me. I have plenty to do, and you need to keep busy before you drive yourself mad with worry. How about some laundry?"

"Honestly, driving myself mad with worry sounds better." My hands still felt a bit slimy from the homemade soap.

Astrid laughed. "You're going to be fine."

23
RYKLIN

IT WAS a grim trip through the woods. My companions didn't speak unless necessary, and we dove for cover at the slightest sound. But we didn't come across any smugglers—or any bodies.

Solara and Rook weren't out there.

It was several miles over hilly terrain to the edge of the camp, and by the time it was in sight, my legs burned with exertion. Nearly five years on a space station had eaten into my endurance, even with a manual labor job. Or perhaps it was the real gravity weighing me down.

The edge of the camp was marked by an unguarded outbuilding. It was little more than a hut with curtained windows and a metal roof. Not secure enough to hold prisoners, certainly, but perhaps there was something in there we could use.

"We need to return." Galen was the leader of this scouting party, and he was looking at me as he spoke. "Most of the original buildings are wired for comms, but the system is probably monitored. The moment you send your message, they'll be on you."

The possibility had occurred to me, but I'd promised my mate that I would return, and nothing would see me break my word. "I'll figure something out."

"Don't lead them back to us." Galen's second in command, Kai, scowled. She wasn't human, but I didn't recognize her species with red skin, horns, and yellow eyes.

"I won't." Noelle was at the encampment; I couldn't let the smugglers find her.

"Let's keep our ears open," said Galen. "I want to return with information." The scouting group melted back into the forest, disappearing with the kind of skill that even I found impressive.

I had no weapon except my claws and no knowledge of the layout of the camp. And that outbuilding was just sitting there waiting to be investigated.

Like a trap.

I was tempted to go inside, my newly awakened

emotions trying to drag my feet across the distance so that I could begin my search. And if I was still soulless, I'd already be there. From where I stood, nothing appeared out of place. It could simply be a little used building sitting at the edge of camp.

But these smugglers knew about the survivors from the mine. They knew they could be a threat. If they didn't need the building, why leave it standing?

I forced myself to skirt around the edge of the camp, waiting for some sign that avoiding the outbuilding was the right move. But it kept standing there, a beacon to my instincts, until I was far enough away to enter the camp from a different path.

I could hear the sound of heavy equipment in the distance. The camp was large. As Astrid had said, at its height, the mine had employed a thousand or so people. But there was no way the smugglers had that many. I doubted they had a hundred, unless they were hiding a large contingent of jailers somewhere.

A dozen. Perhaps two dozen. Enough to turn a profit without needing too many people to keep them captive.

The outer edges of the camp looked abandoned, buildings falling down, the cracked pavement turning to mud in some places. But there were also tire tracks, signs that the smugglers still used the road.

I heard the sound of wheels over pavement just before a truck turned a corner, and I dived for cover, hiding behind a pile of rubble as a large truck rumbled down the way. I couldn't see the driver from my hiding spot or any guards, but I waited in place for several long moments until the truck had cleared me.

I'd never been alone on a mission before. In the Legion, I'd had a team, both before I lost my soul and after. There had been backup, a plan, assurance that if I died, it wouldn't be alone.

No one was coming for me now. So, I had to be more careful than I'd ever been.

I turned Galen's words over. The moment I sent a message, I'd call the whole of the camp down on my position. There would be no running away. And I couldn't count on a quick rescue. If my message got out, it would take time for Drex and the others to gather what they needed for an offensive. And that was provided that station security didn't get in their way.

I wondered if these smugglers had paid off the

station. They must have. Station security was in everyone's pocket.

But I still had my comm. It was useless for getting a message out, the signal not strong enough to reach the ship. But that wasn't what I needed it for. I powered up the device and was thankful the thing hadn't malfunctioned after our dunk in the river.

I had to get a message out, but I didn't need to be there to send it. A recording would do nicely.

I thought through my words carefully. If they had someone monitoring comms, they might be able to quickly jam the signal. But even that took a little time, a few seconds at least. I should be able to send at least one sentence.

I had to make it count.

The first building I searched didn't have anything of use. Nor did the second. Or the third. Hope was a newly born thing in my mind, and it was quickly withering.

But the fourth building had an old-fashioned comms array that responded to my touch when I slid my fingers over the command screen. It was a larger building than the first two. The comms equipment was right in the front, and there was a door that blocked off the rest of the building from sight. I didn't hear any guards, so I decided not to worry about it.

I found the correct frequency and took a deep breath before pulling my own comm out of my pocket. The second I pressed the CONNECT icon, my time would be limited, and I had to run like there were monsters at my feet if I had any hope of making it to safety.

My hands didn't shake. There was no room for nerves now, not if I was going to make it back to my mate.

I pressed the icon and set up the recording.

And that's when I heard the scream coming from the other room.

I hesitated. Running now might see me to safety. Sticking around would surely get me caught.

What would Noelle want me to do?

She wouldn't want me leaving anyone behind. Damn the stars.

The door to the rest of the building was locked, but the lock disengaged when I pressed the button on a panel on the wall. And sitting in a small closet were two tied up humans and one large rat that the male human was staring at with panicked eyes.

The rat didn't seem to care too much about either of them.

"Rook and Solara?" I asked. I couldn't hear foot-
steps pounding our way, not yet, but it was only a
matter of time.

The woman nodded frantically. They were both
tied up with rope, their mouths gagged, though not
well enough to muffle Rook's terrified shriek.

I unsheathed my claws, and Solara looked ready
to fight me, even with her restraints. It took a
moment to get her untied, and then I turned to her
companion. He'd been struggling, and his bonds
were looser, though the skin around his wrists was
all mangled. Discovering them and getting them
free had taken all of three minutes.

Too much time.

"Run for the woods, but don't let them follow
you to camp," I said. I didn't want to free these
people just to bring down the smugglers on Astrid's
people.

"Who are you?" Solara demanded.

"Ryklin. There's no time." Now I could hear
angry men coming our way, and with two trauma-
tized and possibly injured humans, there was no
way they'd make it out of here on their own. I
hurried them out the door and pushed them in front
of me. "Run for all your worth. I'll cover you."

They didn't need more encouragement.

The smuggler's angry running was getting closer. I unsheathed my claws again and wished I had a weapon.

The first blaster shot from the smugglers went wild, sparks lighting up one of the old buildings lining the street. My instincts wanted me to dive for cover, but we couldn't afford to stand and fight. Running was the only chance we had for survival.

I didn't look back. And I didn't see one of the smugglers take aim.

Between one step and the next, pain exploded up and down my back, and I fell to the ground. I couldn't move, but Rook and Solara kept running.

I only hoped it was worth it.

24

NOELLE

Something was wrong.

I didn't panic when the scouts came back. I knew it was possible, probable even, that they'd return without Ryklin. They had a different mission. They'd found no sign of Solara or Rook, and a pall hung over the entire camp.

Astrid tried comforting me, and when that didn't work, she put me on lunch duty to keep my mind occupied. But lunch was over, the camp was fed, and my mate still wasn't back. It was bad enough to think that I might be stuck on Nebula forever, but to be stuck here without my mate was unbearable.

I'd only known for a day—less than that—but already I needed him like the air I breathed.

I needed to find him.

Working lunch duty had given me some information about the storehouses of the camp, and I tried not to feel too guilty as I snuck in. As Astrid said, food wasn't an issue here. They wouldn't miss a few rations or the sack I borrowed to carry them. And if all went well, at least I could return the bag. Besides, Ryklin and I were trying to get Astrid and her people a ticket off of Nebula. They wouldn't need the rations anyway.

"What are you doing?" Astrid caught me stuffing apples into the bag.

Justifying my actions to myself so I don't feel bad about this. I didn't say that. Obviously. "Ryklin should be back by now." I took some day-old bread too. No use hiding what I was doing; I'd already been caught. "I can't just leave him out there."

"He may have been captured. We all knew that was a risk." Her tone was gentle, but her words were cruel.

"I can't just leave him out there. You don't understand." My entire soul was screaming at me to run after him. The fact that I hadn't already was a testament to my willpower and restraint.

"You think you're the first person to lose someone they love?"

Love.

The word blasted through me, echoing down deep.

It was one thing to think about mates, about him calling me denya, about what that meant. But love was what humans called it, how we made our partnerships. It was something built over time, something that grew and flourished as couples grew together.

Could I love him already?

It was so fast, and yet ...

And yet.

"I have to try, Astrid." I slung the straps over my shoulders. The pack wasn't too heavy. I'd only taken enough food for a day or two.

Astrid pursed her lips, and it quickly turned into a grimace. Then she shook her head and reached for one of the packs hanging on a hook on the wall. "Damn it. I can't just let you go alone."

Maybe I should have protested, but having someone who knew the terrain would make finding Ryklin easier.

Because I was going to find him. There was no other option.

Astrid grabbed more apples and bread along with something that looked like jerky that I hadn't noticed. Then she pulled two canteens off a shelf and handed them to me. "Fill these, but don't let anyone see you."

There was a rainwater tank around the back of the storehouse, and I did as she instructed.

Astrid looked a bit conflicted as we snuck out of the camp and into the forest. It was late afternoon, and night would begin to fall soon. No doubt someone would come looking for her. But she hadn't wasted any time telling people where she was going.

"We know that Ryklin made it to the miners camp," Astrid told me as we climbed the ridge that lead to the edge of the camp. "Galen reported back that all was well when he last saw him. It may just be that he's had to hide to escape detection. Or he's chosen to lie low so as not to risk a hike over unfamiliar terrain once night falls." She shot me a look at that.

Okay, fine, maybe not my smartest move, but I was desperate.

"Do you think that's what he's doing?" I asked.

She didn't answer.

And that was answer enough.

We hiked in silence, Astrid's expression growing grimmer with each step. Birds chirped like mad in the trees, and a brave rabbit darted in front of us.

"Will you go back when we get in touch with Nebula Outpost?" I asked. I needed to say something; my mind was going crazy with worry.

"If I could, I'd lay in a hot bath for three hours and then take a shower and do the whole thing again." She sounded wistful. "There's a hot spring about three miles away, but we have to get together a whole party to go there, some people guarding while others bathe, then the other way around. There's never enough time to fully relax. Mostly I just bathe in the river these days."

"So, is that a yes? Do you think anyone would like to stay?" I couldn't imagine it, but some people liked living in nature.

"If we could have some actual medical supplies, maybe a doctor, maybe some real tech, I think some people would definitely stay. And some people living up on the station would want to come down. *If* you can get in touch."

I opened my mouth to insist help was coming when a loud blast rang out behind us.

Astrid dove for the ground and took me with her. We both lay there barely breathing, trying to figure out what was going on.

Another blast came a moment later. I could feel Astrid's flinch.

"That's the camp," she said. "It's under attack."

"Go. Help. I'll be fine." It was getting dark, but we'd taken a flashlight with us. I could do this. I could find Ryklin.

"No, you can't stay out here alone." Her expression was conflicted. "You need to come back with me."

"I'm going to find Ryklin. You can come with me, or you can go back to them, but don't try and stop me." He was in trouble, and he needed my help.

She nodded once, and she clearly wasn't happy about it. "Act quick. If they're attacking us, they may be distracted. Keep walking straight until you see the encampment. It's another mile or so." Then she turned and started running back the way we came.

As her form retreated, I realized just how alone I was.

Go straight. Find Ryklin. Get home.

I could do this. I had to find my mate.

25

RYKLIN

Ropes dug into my skin, rubbing the flesh raw. I'd tried using my claws to rip at the fibers, but the angle was wrong, and all I'd managed to do was rip a stripe out of my own skin. It stung, but I could ignore that pain.

I couldn't ignore the worry and regret clawing at me. Alone in a cell—the same cell I'd broken Solara and Rook out of—all I had were my thoughts and feelings. *Feelings.* Half a decade without a soul had atrophied my ability to recognize all of them, but what else could I do but stew when I was caught there, leaving my mate vulnerable and alone.

They'd beaten me. It was the kind of beating you gave someone when you wanted him to survive. They made me hurt but not enough that they couldn't shove a pickax in my hand tomorrow and send me down a mine shaft. I had to consider that good news. If I was alive, I could escape. All they had to do was lose their focus for a moment, and I'd be a free Detyen.

I could hear whispers of men talking through the door. Some time ago, there'd been a commotion and what sounded like a lot of people leaving. Before I'd lost consciousness, I'd counted a dozen smugglers. If there were more, I hadn't seen them.

"You think he's one of the weird ones?" asked one of my captors.

"You mean like that big one who wouldn't make a noise if you stabbed him?" asked the second.

"Obviously."

"I don't know."

Could they be talking about another soulless Detyen? Had they taken one prisoner? My men and I had been abandoned by our people, slated for death and sent away before the punishment could be meted out. But missions went wrong sometimes, and soldiers got left behind. Especially soulless soldiers. To some of our brethren, we were little better than machinery.

Under other circumstances, I might have made it

a priority to find out, but I couldn't. I needed to get to Noelle, and we needed to get off the planet.

Had my message gone through?

It had been hours, at least, since I tried. If the message had gone through, someone must have heard it. But would they understand the urgency of the situation?

I slumped back against the wall, and my hands smashed behind me, my fingers brushing against the bindings. I extended my claws and tried again, finally snagging just a bit of the rope and tearing at it.

It was slow, tedious work, and the rope bit even harder into my wrists. But it *was* working. My shoulder screamed at me, the angle all wrong and beyond painful, but pain was immaterial compared to freedom.

With a final snap, the rope sagged, and I pulled my hands free, my shoulder in a new kind of agony as I gave it the full range of motion for the first time in hours.

Dealing with the bindings at my feet took only moments, but standing was a slower affair. I took my time. The men beyond the door didn't know I was free. I didn't need to spring right into action.

I needed to get out.

"Who's that?" I heard one of the men ask. But if the other responded, he was too quiet for me to hear.

I needed them to open the door. I didn't think I could break it down from the inside, not without meeting a whole host of smugglers waiting for me with blasters on the other side.

"I need water!" I yelled, trying to make my voice sound a bit hoarse. "Give me some damned water!" I hadn't been given anything since they tied me up. No meal, nothing to drink. If they meant to keep me as a slave, they had to feed me sometime.

Why not now?

"Shut up!" the guard outside the door yelled.

"I'm thirsty." I was, I realized, but I wasn't going to focus on that. "Come on, just give me something to drink."

I heard muttering but couldn't make out the words. It didn't matter. The lock disengaged, and a smuggler stood in the doorway, one hand on his belt buckle. Whether he meant to beat me or worse, I didn't know, and he didn't get a chance to try.

I launched myself at him and raked my claws down his side. Then I finished him off.

It happened in a heartbeat. He didn't have time to scream.

And I was covered in blood.

Unavoidable.

I didn't see the other guard, but the communications array was still there. There was also an old-fashioned modified blaster sitting on the table, probably belonging to the dead guard.

I grabbed it and shoved it in my pocket. Most blasters weren't fatal, but they could be modified to deliver deadly blows. It would even the playing field enough if the smugglers knew I could kill them with both my claws and my gun.

I found the right frequency and sent out a distress signal using an old Detyen code that my men on Nebula Outpost would recognize. I left the message on loop and backed away from the comms station. Someone could be listening in again, and I had to run.

Plus, there was that guard still out there. And maybe the other men, if I hadn't heard them run away from the mining camp. I wanted intel, a team. Instead, I was running blind.

Then I heard a feminine scream, and my vision went red.

I knew that voice.

Would know my mate's voice anywhere.

Someone was hurting her. And I had to make it stop.

<h1 style="text-align:center">26</h1>

<h2 style="text-align:center">NOELLE</h2>

MAKING it into the camp wasn't too hard, but it turned out that stealth was. I hated the evil grin on the smuggler's mouth as he clamped his hand around my arm and tried to drag me somewhere. I struggled, but he was freaking strong.

No matter how hard I hit or struggled, his grip didn't let up. But I had to get out, had to find Ryklin.

Then the smuggler pulled out a knife, and I screamed. His grin grew even more malicious. "Gonna cut up the pretty lady," he crooned.

"Please, don't." He lazily swiped the knife my way, and I jerked back, just out of reach. That only made the smuggler laugh.

Then his eyes widened at something behind me,

and he tried to pull me forward, "Move!" he commanded.

Not a chance in all the hells. I couldn't break out of his grasp, but he couldn't drag me quickly without my help. And if he wanted to move, I was going to stay put. But I didn't dare look behind me to see what was coming our way.

The smuggler swore and yanked me closer, raising the knife to press it to my throat. "One move and the bitch gets it."

"Denya," said a voice so low and dangerous it was like hearing a monster whisper in your ear. I shivered, but it wasn't from fear. I looked up to find my mate standing there, looking feral. He had blood streaking down his torso, but he didn't look injured.

The smuggler stepped back, pulling me with him and slicing the blade lightly across my neck. It stung, and I could feel a warm trickle of blood.

Ryklin growled.

"Let me go, and she's yours," the smuggler said.

Ryklin shook his head, but he didn't move. "She's already mine."

I was. With all my heart I was.

"You're going to die," Ryklin told the man. "You're going to take your last breath, and then she's going to be free."

"I'll take her with—" He dropped, the knife falling out of his hand as his skin smoked from a blaster shot I hadn't seen coming.

Ryklin rushed forward and pulled me into his arms. "Denya, are you alright?"

"Fine. I'm fine." I nuzzled my face into his chest and breathed in the scent of my mate. "Are you okay?" He was the reason I was here. My encounter with the smugglers was only a few minutes long; they'd had him for hours. And he was covered in blood.

"Yes." But his hand was shaking where it rested against my back, the tips of his claws scratching gently at my spine.

"The blood?"

"Not mine. Mine would be green." And the blood soaking into his clothes was dark and red. Human.

Maybe I should have been more concerned about him killing people, but there was a bruise blooming on my wrist, and I'd heard the stories Astrid told us. If anyone deserved it, it was these smugglers.

I ran my hand down the mostly clean parts of his shirt, needing to reassure myself that he was all here in one piece. I touched his cheek, and he leaned into it, pressing a kiss to the palm of my hand. I slid my other hand through his hair and felt some sort of tension I hadn't known was there release.

He held me as though he was afraid if he let go, he'd never hold me again.

But we were in the middle of the smugglers camp, and Astrid and her people were under attack. I forced myself to step back. "Did you find comms? Did you send a message?"

"Yes. If they heard it, they'll come."

That was a big if, given the people that had been stranded here for a decade.

"Astrid was coming with me, but someone attacked the village. We have to go help." If we ran, it would still take the better part of an hour to get back. Would they still be holding out?

"I think I heard most of the smugglers head out awhile ago. Let's take a minute, try and find some weapons or a vehicle. We need to be smart about this." He was all soldier now.

I was still just a mechanic. I'd never even held a blaster.

But Ryklin took one out of the holster of the man he'd killed, the one who'd held a knife to my neck, and handed it over. "It's simple enough. Point and hit the trigger. Don't point it at anyone you don't want to hit. Watch the charge level on the handle.

It'll recharge automatically, but if you fire too much, it could overheat. Got it?"

"Uh, sure?" I didn't sound confident.

"Shoot that building." He pointed towards a wall on the opposite side of the street.

"What did that building ever do to you?" My hand was shaky as I raised it up, but I hit the trigger, and a blast of red light shot out and scorched a mark near the door. Not *quite* where I'd been aiming, but Ryklin didn't need to know that.

"Now you've shot a blaster. Got it?"

"I guess." I would have happily taken another week's worth of lessons before running off into battle, but we didn't have the luxury.

And we didn't know who was still lurking in the mining camp. Neither of us wanted to go much deeper in. If there were prisoners, there would be guards. And though my heart hurt at the thought of the people there, we didn't have the force to free them.

Not yet.

But once we were back home on Nebula Outpost, I'd do everything in my power to see these smugglers stopped and these people freed.

Not that I had much power.

We found an old two-seater power bike and

climbed on. It sputtered to life and limped for the first few meters, but then something in the engine turned over, and the ride was smooth as Ryklin navigated us through the dark forest with only the dim headlamp in front of us.

I would have gotten us lost in a minute. Good thing I'd found my soldier to lead us back.

The bike was faster than running, and we could hear the sounds of battle as we crested the hill that led into the encampment.

I was scared we'd find a smoking ruin. There was definitely smoke, but the survivors were fighting back.

The first body we saw was of a dead smuggler. The next three were wearing clothes from the encampment, though I hadn't seen them alive. Ryklin stopped the bike before we drove into the heart of the fighting.

"You need to find cover," he said, face serious. "I'm going to end this."

I wanted to argue. These people had helped me as much as they'd helped him. Surely I could be useful. I had a blaster! But I wasn't a soldier, and Ryklin was right.

I pulled him close and kissed him. It was brief

and fierce, and it promised more as soon as we got through this. "Come back to me."

"Always." And then he was off.

I was on the edge of the encampment, and while the bodies were proof there'd been fighting, it had moved on from there. But the camp wasn't big, and I could hear screams and cries as people fought.

How long could it last?

I almost tripped over Astrid's body and had to clamp a hand to my mouth to keep from crying out.

Then I saw her chest rise and fall, just a bit. Just enough. She was alive. Clinging to life there at the edge. But she needed medical assistance, and we didn't even have any med gel.

We were in the middle of the walking path. If any of the smugglers came that way, they'd see us. But I couldn't just leave Astrid there after she'd given us so much help. But you weren't supposed to move someone when they were injured, right?

I really wished I'd kept up with the first aid training, and it would be on my list of things to do when I got home. I even made a silent promise to the gods about it. Promises weren't going to help me now.

Blood was pumping sluggishly out of a wound on her side. There was a shack on the other side of the path. If we could make it there, there might be supplies, and there would definitely be cover.

Decision made, I hooked my arms under Astrid's armpits and began to drag her, wincing as she moaned in pain. But at least that meant she was alive. I tried to take comfort in that, but I hated to cause pain.

The shack was bare inside, not a strip of fabric to be found. With no better idea, I stripped off my own top and used a jagged piece of wood to tear the fabric. It was harder than I expected, the fabric hardy. I bunched some of it up and used it as a pad while I wrapped the ragged strips around Astrid's torso.

Then I reached for my blaster, ready to guard the door against anyone who might try to come for us.

Except it wasn't in my pocket.

I peeked onto the path and saw it glinting on the ground, the metal reflected in the moonlight. I didn't want any of the smugglers picking it up, and no one seemed to be around. I had to risk running for it.

Taking a deep breath to steady myself, I darted onto the path and scooped it up. The night was chilly, especially with only a bar on the upper half of my body.

The sounds of fighting had quieted. Was it over now? Dying down? Who was winning?

I was supposed to stay under cover, but with the blaster in my hand, I felt just a little invincible. I crept just a bit farther down the path, keeping as best as I could to the shadows, but trying to see what was going on.

And that was when I saw Ryklin fall limply to the ground.

27
RYKLIN

The bastard saw me go down and thought he had me. I forgot the grim satisfaction that came from tricking the enemy.

He took two steps closer, and I fired, hitting him in the center of his chest. He went down, and I sprang up, ready to face whoever was next. Except no one came at me.

The smell of death and destruction hung heavy in the encampment. Several shacks had been destroyed, and the central brick oven was heavily damaged as both the smugglers and survivors had used it for cover at different points in the battle.

Galen approached. "We've got two cornered, but the rest are dead, or they've fled." He carried a large rifle that must have been taken off a dead smuggler.

The survivors had started this fight with little more than spears and ingenuity, but they were the ones left standing.

"How many attacked?" I'd killed two and seen another dead.

"About a dozen. I think they finally got tired of us."

I felt some shift in the air and looked behind Galen. Noelle came running, wearing only her trousers and a bra. She wrapped me tight in her arms and didn't let go.

Not that I would let her.

"I saw you go down," she said, her lips brushing against my neck.

I tightened my grip, anger and worry warring. "You were supposed to stay hidden."

She pulled back just enough to look up at me and then over at Galen. "Astrid's hurt badly. I bandaged her as best as I could, but she needs a doctor, or at least some med gel. Do you have anything?"

"No." Galen's expression was stricken. "We can stitch her up. Clean the wound. And then ..."

"She's lost a lot of blood." Noelle stepped back from my embrace, and I felt the loss.

She led us to the shack where she'd left Astrid,

and we acquired more people, Davis and others I didn't know. There was no curtain to act as a door to this shack, and I spotted Astrid's hair before I saw the rest of her. Her skin was deathly pale, and she moaned weakly. The remnants of Noelle's top were tied around her chest in a makeshift bandage. And blood was still leaking around the side of it.

Davis fell to his knees beside her and took her hand. "Astrid ..." He sounded broken.

Galen nodded for me to follow him outside. Noelle went with. "That woman has held us together for the last ten years." His voice was firm. "If it wasn't for her, we'd all be dead or slaves to those smugglers. She can't die."

"Maybe there are supplies back at the miners camp?" Noelle guessed, her brows drawn down in worry. "Do you think there are many of them left back there waiting?"

"We did kill two more," I reminded her. "Whoever's back there is probably guarding their prisoners. And we have real weapons now."

"They rode here in two six-seater vehicles," said Galen. "Only one of those vehicles was destroyed."

"Then get your team together and gather as many weapons as you can. We leave as soon as I join you."

Galen nodded and ran for the center of the encampment.

"Let me go alone." I wasn't begging my mate, not quite. But the thought of her running into danger made my entire being feel unsteady. "It's probably safe enough. We're going for medical supplies. We'll be back in an hour."

She reached out and clutched my hand. "If you get captured again, I am going to be so pissed. You will never hear the end of it."

I kissed her, pouring every bit of promise I had into the touch of our lips. She tasted like the forest and something sweet, something entirely mine. I could get lost in the kiss forever.

But Astrid was bleeding out in the shack, and we were running out of time.

Noelle ran to find better bandages, and I took off to meet Galen. I didn't see her again before I climbed into the vehicle with Galen's team, and we were off.

It was a bumpy ride back to the mining camp until the driver figured out how to engage the anti-grav. After that, it only took a few minutes to clear the forest and make it to the mining camp. We were all braced for battle. I was waiting by my window with my rifle, ready to shoot anyone that threatened us. Galen was at the other window ready to do the same.

But no one was waiting.

We parked the vehicle and climbed out, heading straight for the heart of the camp. There was no use checking the outbuildings; they would have been stripped of anything useful years ago.

They'd keep their medical supplies to treat the smugglers and their slaves in the most secure part of the camp.

That was the plan.

Then I saw the transport.

I raised my hand, calling for a halt, even as my ears tickled with the sounds of fighting at the center of the camp. It sounded like the prisoners were fighting their captors. And no backup was coming.

"This is a ground to air transport, we can use it to take Astrid up to Nebula Outpost, get her a doctor." And it could get me and Noelle out of there. The transport was relatively small. That still meant it could probably fit every survivor in the encampment and then some.

I could see Galen making the same calculation in his eyes. Then he looked towards the sound of the struggle. "Get her up there. Then come back for us."

He waved his people on, and they took off running towards the struggle to back up the prisoners.

I climbed into the pilot's seat and powered the ship up. It was low on charge, which was probably why it was sitting here, but it would have enough power to get us to Nebula Outpost, especially with a light load.

I hoped.

I had to navigate by sight to get back to the encampment, and I landed on the very edge of the settlement, careful not to set down on anything too important. Several survivors had pilfered rifles aimed at me as I climbed out of the cockpit with my hands raised. When they saw me, most of them lowered their weapons.

Most.

"I'm getting Astrid to a doctor!" That got the rest of them to stand down.

And before I could even go looking, Davis, Noelle, and two others came jogging with Astrid on a makeshift stretcher. I hopped back into the cockpit to open the bay door for them to load her up. Davis and one of the stretcher bearers climbed back out of the cargo bay leaving Noelle with Astrid and a woman who's name I didn't know.

I wanted my mate with me that second, but I

forced myself to keep my cool as I closed the bay door and launched the transport into the sky.

And once we were in range of Nebula Outpost, I broadcast a message on the comms. "I am a resident of Nebula Outpost, and I have an injured woman with me. She needs immediate medical attention."

And this time I was sure they were listening.

28

NOELLE

We were the most popular people on Nebula Outpost, at least as far as station security was concerned.

Someone had given me a top, so at least there was that, but Ryklin was still covered in that smuggler's blood. Astrid was in the medbay with Alice, the woman who'd come with her from the encampment. I was sure they'd be asked every question in the book once Astrid was conscious.

And she would regain consciousness. She had to.

Nebula Outpost couldn't give the best medical care the galaxy had to offer. It was just a small space station on the edge of nowhere. But the doctors and medbots were competent. Astrid would be fine.

I hoped.

"You're trying to tell me that people survived the mining explosion and have been living there for ten years?" The security guard was highly skeptical.

"Alice could tell you more. I literally just met them yesterday." Someone was off corroborating the fact that two escape pods had launched two days ago, and another person was confirming that Ryklin and I both were residents of Nebula Outpost.

I just wanted this to be over.

But it went on for hours. It had to be the middle of the night; my eyes were scratchy and dry, and I was about to slump in my seat. There was nothing more I could tell them.

And finally, they seemed to realize that. The leader of this security group came into the room. "You're free to go right now. We'll contact you when we have more questions."

"And you'll send someone down to retrieve everyone on Nebula? Those smugglers were holding people as prisoners and mining illegally." I didn't want to just leave them there, even if I was happy to be home.

"We have no intention of leaving innocent people trapped on the planet," he assured me.

But I was beginning to understand Nebula

Outpost station security, and I'd be checking on that. A lot.

Ryklin was waiting for me in the hallway. Had it really only been two days since we crashed down on Nebula? Almost three now. I could freak out about how fast I'd fallen for the guy, or I could wrap my arms around him and just be happy that he was mine.

I chose that option.

His clothes were crusty with dried blood, and we both needed to bathe immediately, but I didn't let go for several moments. And then I took his hand and led him to my quarters.

We passed by Pippa and Drex's room, and I spared half a thought for them. Had they realized we were gone?

They could wait until later.

I wanted to get my hands on my mate, but we were both covered in grime and other people's blood. And my shower wasn't big enough for two. Ryklin, ever the gentleman, insisted I bathe myself first. And I would be lying if I said I didn't spend a few extra minutes under the stream of hot water, reveling in the tech.

Astrid was right to miss hot water on demand. I hope she got her three-hour-long bath.

I slipped on a robe and left my clothes in a pile. There was no saving them. They'd be bound for the incinerator.

Ryklin's eyes went red with passion when he saw me all nice and clean. But he kept himself away, as if afraid to get his dirt on me. Probably fair. I was going to take him the moment he got out of the shower.

Then I realized there were no clothes in my quarters for him to wear.

My alien boyfriend was going to have to walk around naked until I fixed that.

Another problem for later.

I grinned and lay back on the bed. I couldn't wait to have my way with my mate, to feel him filling me up and taking me, claiming me, keeping me now that we were safe. There was nothing I could want more.

I didn't realize I fell asleep until I woke up.

I faintly heard the bustle of the hallway outside. It was late in the morning. Unsurprising since we arrived back in the middle of the night. My body felt kind of strange, trying to adjust back to the false gravity of Nebula Outpost. I wasn't sure if I liked that feeling or not.

What I loved was waking up to the hulking alien snoring softly beside me.

Ryklin looked different in sleep, relaxed in a way he never could manage while he was awake. The lines around his mouth had softened; his forehead was completely smooth. He looked at peace.

I shouldn't disturb it. Now would be the perfect time to go get some clothes for him. I wasn't sure where his quarters were, but Drex would doubtlessly have something he could borrow. Ryklin was a bit bigger, but it would work for today.

I kept looking at my mate. Then I trailed my fingers lightly over his lips.

Ryklin reached up and clamped his hand around my wrist, his mouth tugging into a wicked smile. "Didn't anyone ever warn you not to wake a sleeping warrior?" Then he tugged me forward, and I landed on top of him with a yelp.

Our bodies lined up perfectly. I could feel him thickening between us, and my blood began to heat in response. My hips rolled, and I heard Ryklin groan, even as he shifted his legs underneath me, lifting me and putting us at better angles.

Then we were kissing, and it was everything I'd ever wanted. We had time now for lazy, exploratory kisses, the kind you only gave when you weren't on a desperate trek for your life. Ryklin knew what he was doing with his mouth, and I leaned into it, luxuriating in the feeling of his arms around me and the evidence of his arousal pressed tight against me.

"I was going to go find you some clothes," I gasped, my lips dragging across his.

"Why would I need clothes?" He arched up his hips to punctuate the question.

I moaned.

He laid me back on the bed and started to kiss his way down my body. Everywhere his mouth touched, I felt the caress of fire. His hands smoothed along my sides as he untied my robe. He nipped lightly at my belly and my hip bones, driving me insane. I threaded my fingers through his hair and urged him lower, aching for his mouth on my core.

And he obliged.

Ryklin feasted on me with a moan of pure pleasure that only drove me higher. I writhed beneath his mouth as he sucked and licked, alternating between tiny teasing licks and the hard swipes of his tongue. He was going to drive me insane with want.

Not that I was complaining.

My fingers curled in the sheets and in his hair. His hands slid down, and I felt one of his fingers thrust inside of me. His rhythm matched his tongue, and I arched off the bed with a cry.

There were words in there somewhere, but I was too far gone to know what I was saying. Not that Ryklin seemed to mind. He growled against my skin and worked me faster and harder, my body wound so tight I was afraid it would snap.

But Ryklin showed no mercy. I shattered.

The world went white, and I heard myself shout, a wild cry that could probably be heard through the walls.

Ryklin's tongue continued to lap at me, gentling me as he slowly brought me down.

When I was back in my body, he was nipping lightly at my thighs and the flesh around my core.

I was shaking from aftershocks and still my body heated again in anticipation of the main event.

I crooked a lazy, satisfied finger at my man. "Come up here. I need you now."

Ryklin surged up the bed and hovered over me. His eyes blazed red with emotion, and he looked just a bit possessed. I'd made this man look like this.

I reveled in it.

"You are mine," he growled. His mouth captured mine in a branding kiss, and I melted. He was going to consume me, and I welcomed it.

Ryklin pressed his length against my opening, and then he slid in, stretching me in a delicious way that I'd come to love. I savored the feeling as he seated himself inside me and began to move, one arm bracing himself over me as his other hand captured my thigh and wrapped my leg around his waist, changing the angle and allowing him to thrust even deeper.

I groaned as he rubbed against sensitive nerve endings that hadn't yet recovered from my first orgasm. My nails raked down his back, and I was rewarded with his answering growl.

I lifted up enough to press kisses to his shoulder and his neck, biting down on the tender skin. "You are mine," I echoed his claim, needing to say it. "Never going to let you go."

Ryklin shifted his angle so that he was pressing against my clit with each thrust, working me back up towards a peak I'd never expected to climb.

His eyes stayed locked on mine as his hips moved faster, almost out of control. He looked fierce and beautiful above me, all rippling muscle and taut skin.

"Never," he said.

I could only gasp as he claimed me again and again. My body tightened in preparation. And then he shifted position again, just enough so that he could lean down and rain kisses down my neck as he pumped into me.

I cried out again as I came, my nails digging into his skin so hard that I was certain I left marks.

Ryklin groaned his satisfaction, and then I felt his teeth nipping at my throat, breaking the skin and marking me. It stung for just a moment before the heat began to spread, warmth radiating down my body as the bond we'd already sealed seemed to glow with satisfaction.

Ryklin lifted his head, and I pulled his mouth down to mine.

I was going to kiss this man forever.

29
RYKLIN

Leaving my mate in her quarters was the hardest thing I'd ever done. She was asleep, soft and satisfied, and I wanted to take her again and again.

And again.

My body roared with need, and I could see the reflected desire in her eyes. But there were things to settle before we could begin the rest of our lives, and even though my emotions were newly awakened, I could tell that this was something that needed to be done as quickly as possible to keep from putting it off for good.

It would be awkward, though.

Noelle had ordered a simple set of clothes in my size from one of the shops on the station, and they'd been delivered. The pants were a bit snug, and the shirt was tight against the muscles of my chest, but from the way my denya's eyes lit up, I had a feeling I'd be wearing this size from now on.

Anything for her.

My journey wasn't long to my destination, just two doors down. It was the middle of the day now, and it was possible that Drex and Pippa would both be at work. But Drex answered when I knocked. His eyes flicked up and down, taking in my attire, and they widened slightly. For the past four and a half years, I'd worn variations of gray, black, and dark blue. And all of it had been bulky, allowing for ease of movement.

My crimson shirt was a departure.

"May I come in?" I asked. "We need to talk."

Drex opened the door wider and allowed me to step in. He nodded towards the couch, and I sat. He took the chair opposite. The room was more or less identical to Noelle's and twice as big as the room Drex and I had shared with Thalor.

He sat silently, waiting for me to speak. He might have had his emotions back, but I assumed habits of being soulless died hard.

Or he wanted to make me suffer.

I wouldn't wallow in it or make this worse than it was.

"I owe you an apology," I said. "I am sorry for trying to kill you and for not believing you about Pippa."

There was a low growl in the back of Drex's throat when I said her name. I hadn't laid a hand on her, but I'd been a threat all the same. I could see that now.

"You said you were leaving the station."

I almost smiled at that. I could feel the twitch at the side of my mouth. And Drex must have seen something. His eyes narrowed. "Have you heard what happened?" I asked. Rumors had a way of spreading quickly, but we hadn't even been back a full day yet, and I had a feeling station security would want to keep this as quiet as they could.

"I heard something about survivors on Nebula. Pippa's parents—"

"Didn't make it." I wouldn't let that hope linger. "Noelle and I found the survivors on Nebula. She's my denya."

His eyebrows went up, and his mouth stayed closed.

"Do you have anything to say about that?" I didn't know what the strange emotion making my heart beat erratically was. I didn't like it, though.

The ground under me felt uncertain, even though I was sitting down.

Emotions weren't all great.

Drex was silent for several more seconds. Then he reached into his pocket and pulled out his communicator. "I think it's time we spoke to the others about this. Once was a fluke. Twice is ... something else." He typed out a message and sent it. My communicator had been lost somewhere on Nebula, and I'd need to get a new one. And see about getting my job back. There was much to consider.

"Congratulations," Drex said after another few moments. "I hope you're happy."

"I am."

We sat in silence while we waited for our comrades to come to Drex's quarters. Nebula Outpost was a big station, and it took nearly an hour for the last of them—Jorin—to get there. Thalor, Zyrus, Kaelor, and Jorin all remained standing, faces neutral as they looked between Drex and me.

How had we lived like that for so long? Was it even living?

I'd had some doubts about the soulless procedure before I agreed to undergo it, but ultimately I thought it was my duty to the Detyen Legion and our warriors. But perhaps it had always been a mistake, some sinister bargain that turned soldiers into automatons and doctors into monsters.

We were a long way from the Detyen Legion now and had no say in what they did. But that did little to assuage my doubts.

"Ryklin has news," Drex announced before nodding towards me.

Four heads turned my way, posture straight, poised to receive orders and carry them out.

It was eerie. Had it always been eerie or was I only noticing it now that I had my emotions back?

It didn't matter.

"I've found my denya," I told them. There was no reaction from the four soulless former warriors, but Drex leaned forward in his seat just a bit. I gave them the briefest summary of my time on Nebula Outpost as I could, but it still took longer than expected.

It was Zyrus who spoke first when I was done. "Do you think it was your proximity to your denya that brought your emotions back?"

His question surprised me. When Drex changed, I'd been convinced he'd fixated on Pippa and would be a threat to us all. Nothing in me could have believed what he said was true. Yet Zyrus had. Zyrus *did*. And it was almost like he was curious, even if that was impossible. "I believe so," I said.

Drex nodded in agreement.

He didn't ask about fixation. It had been a grave concern of mine, but I was beginning to wonder just how real it was. What if the fixated had found their mates? Perhaps not all of them, but some. What if the Legion had been killing soldiers who could be healed?

"Fixation is still a risk," I said, even if I was beginning to have doubts. "You still must be on your guard. But Drex and I prove that sometimes there is another path. If you have any questions, if you suspect that you may have found your denya but aren't sure, talk to Drex or me. Perhaps we can help." It was tempting to ask them to report to us, to step into the roll of monitoring them for deviation.

But until a few days ago, I'd been one of them. And this was not the Legion. I would not be their jailer or executioner, not unless they actually crossed a line. They deserved their freedom, as much as they could ever have.

"Is it safe to stay on Nebula Outpost?" Kaelor asked. "This revelation about the survivors will bring attention to the station, and there has been a noticeable rise in crime. What if the Legion sends someone here to investigate?"

"Investigate what?" asked Drex. "I don't think a few Solar Flare dealers are going to know anything about the destruction of Detya. The Legion has no reason to come here. But, of course, no one will stop you from leaving, if you think that is the wisest option."

Kaelor nodded but didn't say anything else.

The soulless filed out, but Zyrus was last to go, and he hesitated. "What did you say the woman's name was? The one you brought with you?"

"Astrid was injured. Alice came as her companion." It was a strange question. He could have no connection to Nebula, but I saw no reason to keep the information from him.

He nodded and left.

Drex and I exchanged a glance.

Zyrus's curiosity would be something to watch.

30
NOELLE

THE DETYENS HAD COMMANDEERED Pippa's quarters, but since she was basically squeeing in joy and bouncing up and down on one of my chairs with her hands clasped together and a look of absolute glee on her face, I didn't think she minded.

"Oh my god, you and Ryklin! That's so ... obvious. That whole ... thing ... makes sense now." I thought she was going to lunge forward and hug me.

"You mean the stalking thing?" I was beyond happy with my mate. I really was. But I wasn't just going to let that part go. He was going to be teased about it for the rest of his very long life.

"Whatever." Pippa waved the concern away. "Besides, if he hadn't been stalking you, you never would have had bonding time alone down on Nebula." Her smile faded a bit at the mention of the planet.

Her parents had died in the explosion, and I'd had to reopen that wound when I told her about the survivors. I thought that her exuberance about Ryklin and me might have been a bit exaggerated to plaster over the fresh pain.

I was tempted to apologize, as if I'd done something wrong by finding Astrid and her people, but Pippa wouldn't like that.

"If Ryklin had been thinking clearly, he might have sent a message to station security before he chased after me."

"Yeah, cause they're who I'd count on in a crisis." She snorted.

I had to agree. Give me a Detyen any day.

Pippa's communicator beeped, and she checked the screen before cursing. "I've got a meeting to get to. Have you told Rexal what's going on?" Mr. Rexal was our boss. He was a normally accommodating man, so hopefully I'd still have a position when he found out I'd had no choice but to miss a few shifts.

"I set up a meeting with him for tomorrow morning." I was still bone tired today, even with a full night's sleep and an invigorating wake up. Hopefully I'd be in better shape for my meeting.

Clearly my friend didn't want to go, but I shooed her out of the room. No use putting her job at risk.

When was Ryklin coming back?

I tapped my toes impatiently against the floor and traced my finger over the fabric of my sofa. My skin felt buzzy with tired energy, and I needed to do something. And my mate wasn't there to help me out.

Leaving the room wasn't so much a conscious decision as it was just something to do. I didn't know where I was going until I was nearly to the entrance of the medical wing. I slipped past the receptionist. I was sure no one would be allowed back to see Astrid, but what the receptionist didn't know wouldn't hurt me.

I peeked in through the windows of every room I passed. The medical wing was mostly for serious cases. Usually, if you were injured, they gave you a portable medbot and sent you back to your quarters after the initial healing. It was only those on the brink of death or those who required more extensive healing that stayed there.

I saw Alice sitting beside a bed and knew I'd found the right room.

I slipped in, and Alice shot up from her seat, putting herself in front of Astrid's prone body, her expression fierce. It cleared when she saw me. We hadn't spoken much down on Nebula, but she clearly knew who I was.

"Is everything alright?" I asked as Alice settled down into her seat.

Astrid's chest rose and fell evenly, and I felt a bit of tension release. She was alive. Her color was better. She'd make it through this.

Alice glanced towards the door and kept her voice low. "Station security said they'd post a guard on the door. Just in case. He was there for a few hours, and I fell asleep. When I woke up, he was gone. No one's come back since."

"Did you ask about it?" That didn't sound great.

"I tried to ask the doctor, but she said that this area is plenty secure, and there's nothing to worry about."

"Are you worried about something specific?" We'd made it safely back. I couldn't think of any threat. "We're going to make sure they get everyone from the planet. No one's going to be stuck there." I'd make it happen if I had to fund the damned project myself. What was the point of having rich parents back home if I didn't use their money every now and then?

"She's not worried about that." Astrid's voice was weak but welcome. Her eyes blinked open, and she looked at me with a smile. "Do I have you to thank for these digs?"

"Among others." I'd give her the full story once she recovered. "What's Alice worried about, then?"

Alice gave Astrid's hand a squeeze. "I'll go tell the doctor you're awake." She left the two of us alone.

Astrid waited until the door slid closed to talk. "We've all had ten years to think about what would happen if someone ever rescued us," she said. She coughed a little, and I handed her a glass of water, which she sipped. "There have to be people on this station who've known we're down there. There's no way they've missed all the smuggling ships. So, either palms were greased or there are people here straight up in on it. And if they think any of us can ID them ..."

"You think someone on this station will try to hurt you." Not a question.

"Either smugglers or security for the mining company. We're a long way from anywhere, and it will take awhile for news to travel. But I don't think they're going to like the idea of the world learning they left over a hundred people stranded for a decade. Imagine the possible payouts if we can find a court to take our case. They left us to die once; I don't see how killing us makes much of a differ- ence." She sighed. "I'll feel a lot better when everyone is safe up here. Maybe I'm just paranoid."

"Maybe." But at least part of what she said felt very possible. "Ryklin has men he trusts. They're trained warriors. And they have no reason to want to harm you or your people. How about one of them guards you until things settle down? Believe me, they're better than station security."

"That doesn't sound terrible."

I stood. The doctor would be coming soon, and I didn't want to get caught in the room. "I'll talk to Ryklin. I'm sure you and Alice will be set up with a place to stay soon. We'll keep you safe."

"You better." She was smiling as she said it, but the threat hung over us.

I hoped I hadn't rescued Astrid only to bring her into more danger.

Ryklin was waiting for me when I got back to my quarters, and he swept me up into his arms and covered my mouth in a toe-curling kiss before I even got the door shut.

"I missed you too," I said as he set me down. "How did talking with your guys go?"

He pulled me close and nuzzled my neck. "We can talk later." He rained tiny kisses along my collarbone. "I have plans for you."

That sent a bolt of heat right through me, but the fear I'd seen deep in Astrid's expression kept me on task. "Someone needs to guard Astrid until all of this settles down. One of your men. I don't trust station security."

Ryklin put a little distance between us, and I tried not to be disappointed. "You think she's in danger?"

"She thinks she's in danger. I'm not so sure. But considering all the help she gave us, I figured it wouldn't hurt to help her out. Do you think one of your guys could do it? Would they?" I understood that they were like Ryklin before he'd met me, cold and emotionless. But they were trained warriors and fully capable of the job.

I hoped.

"I'll ask. We won't let anything happen to her. You have my word."

"Good. Very good."

And with that settled, I launched myself into his arms and tackled him to the bed.

31
ZYRUS

I WATCHED the human woman limp down the hallway, her dark hair pulled back into a messy bun and her face pale from her stay in the hospital wing.

Was she beautiful? Would she be when she was fully recovered?

I'd known that, once, I was sure. I could tell beauty in a glance or learn to appreciate its more complex presentations after study. Now? Nothing. There'd been nothing for six years, four months, and twenty-seven days.

I'd never asked if other soulless Detyens tracked the time from their procedure. I doubted they did. Why would it matter? At most, it would track the time to my likely demise. Few soulless made it longer than seven years.

And here I was, heading straight for that cliff.

I'd already faced that death once, when I'd second guessed an officer's order that would have lead me into certain death.

And in a way, I'd died the day I went under the knife and let them remove my soul.

All for the minute hope that one day I might meet her again.

Now she was standing in front of me, and she didn't recognize me.

It was only fair, I supposed. I could see her with my eyes, but there was no deeper recognition, not the soul deep certainty I'd once experienced the first time we'd met eleven years ago.

Did I look so different?

She hadn't changed a bit. Except for the scar on her face.

"So, you're going to be my bodyguard?" Astrid asked. "I think this is my room." We were just down the hall from Noelle and Pippa.

I didn't tell Astrid this room belonged to a woman who had been murdered not too long ago. People with emotions could be weird about such things. It was just a space; it held no echoes of the terrible things that had happened there.

"Yes," I said. "I will make sure nothing happens to you."

"Do you have a name? Noelle didn't mention it." She smiled up at me, though there was a bit of a wince in it. The pain from her injury must have not been fully healed.

"Zyrus."

Her eyes narrowed then, and she took a closer look. "Zyrus ..." She stepped forward, but before she could go any farther, she jerked her hand back and stepped back. "Nice to meet you. And thank you."

"You don't have to thank me."

I'd do anything to protect his mate. Even if she didn't know who he was.

32

RYKLIN

H‌AD I set it up right? Prepared for every contingency?

It had been a long time since I prepared for battle, and I'd never been as nervous for that as I was for tonight. Everything had to be perfect.

Some men might have waited for a special occasion of some kind, an anniversary marking our mating or the first time we'd met, anything really. But I didn't need to wait for some special day to show my denya how special she was.

I would have done this in our quarters, but I wanted something bigger, better. And this tiny observation deck was just the spot. I'd managed to reserve it for personal use and snuck in two meals. Technically people weren't supposed to eat in there, but we couldn't have a romantic dinner without food.

The table was set, the candles were lit, I'd even splurged on a bottle of wine.

So where was my mate?

Her shift had ended more than an hour ago, and she'd had plenty of time to shower and read the note I'd left for her. I'd even asked Pippa to steer her in this direction just in case they got to talking after work.

Impatience.

I was working to identify the emotions as they came. It was strange sometimes, what had once been so natural now sometimes fit like a too-tight sweater. And not in the way my mate liked me wearing too-tight clothes.

But I would deal with all the nervousness and impatience I had to for one moment of the joy I experienced when Noelle walked into the room.

And when she did, it made all the waiting worth it.

She saw me first, and then the spread, and her eyes widened. "We're not supposed to eat in here!" She quickly shut the door behind her.

"I won't tell if you won't." I'd once been a stickler for the rules, but I was finding it ... fun ... to break them sometimes. Especially when it made my mate look at me like *that*.

"What's going on? Why all this?" She took a seat and accepted a glass of wine.

I sat next to her and presented our plates. It wasn't much, just some prepared meals from her favorite restaurant on the station and a small cake I'd ordered especially for tonight. "I wanted to do something for you."

"Is this to apologize for the whole stalking thing?" She raised a single eyebrow and looked at me.

"Would I know your favorite cake if I hadn't stalked you?" At that point, the only way to react to the accusations of stalking was to fire right back. She'd forgiven me, I knew, but I'd never live it down.

"There's cake?" She grinned. "You're forgiven. For tonight."

"Then I suppose I'll need to figure out something to help you forgive me tomorrow." I punctuated that with a kiss.

Noelle leaned into it, tasting faintly of wine and the small bite of cake she'd already taken. "I bet we can think of something." Her hand landed on my thigh, and I grinned into our kiss.

I looked forward to earning my mate's forgiveness every night for the rest of our lives.

Thank you for reading Intrepid Bond!
I'd appreciate it so much if you would consider leaving a review.

The Detyen Warrior Outcast series will continue.

NEED A BIT MORE OF INTREPID BOND?

Sign up at the link below to **receive a free bonus epilogue!**

Find out now!
https://katerudolph.net/index.php/intrepid-bond-bonus/

———

Looking for EVEN MORE alien romance?

Detyens are doomed to die young if they don't find their fated mates.

Could humans be the answer to their prayers?

When Ruwen meets Lis, a human woman on the run from her nasty alien abductors their story changes the fate of a doomed alien race...

Journey into the world of **Mated to the Alien** where you'll find fierce women, protective heroes, fated mates, and a galaxy big enough to blow your mind!

Learn more

WHAT TO READ NEXT
RUWEN

Ru's species is cursed. He'll be dead by his next birthday if he doesn't find his mate...

Ruwen knows he's a goner. His alien species is cursed by a deadly genetic quirk and he'll be dead before the month is out, unless he finds his fated mate. She's the only woman in the universe who can save him. It's too bad that most Detyen women are dead. But could he find hope with a human?

Abducted, ditched, and on the run from vicious aliens...

After being kidnapped from Earth by unknown foes, Lis has been dropped on a inhospitable planet with little food and no hope. She'll do anything to find a ship to take her back to Earth, but Polai is hostile to all alien life, and Lis is running out of places to hide. Can she trust the alien who looks at her with heat in his eyes?

An impossible chance...

From the moment he sees her, Ru knows Lis is his mate. But she's already wounded and distrustful of aliens. How can he prove that he's trustworthy? If he can't overcome Lis's fears, their bond will break before it has a chance to form, leaving Ru dead and Lis all alone in a hostile galaxy.

Get your copy

ALSO BY KATE RUDOLPH

Detyen Warrior Outcasts
Fated Mate Alien Romance
These doomed warriors were abandoned by their people and live on the edge. Their mates hold the key to their salvation.
Pick a book and jump into the action today!

Dangerous Bond
Intrepid Bond

———

Mated to the Alien
Fated Mate Alien Romance

Detyens are doomed to die young if they don't find their fated mates.

Follow along as these mated pairs fight off aliens, corrupt dictators, prejudiced humans, pirates, and more! The books can be read or listened to in any order, though some characters show up in multiple stories.

Select books available in audio.

Pick a book and jump into the action today!

Ruwen

Tyral

Stoan

Cyborg

Krayter

Kayleb

Shayn

Braxtyn

Doryan

Dekon

———

Detyen Warriors

Detya was destroyed a hundred years ago. These doomed warriors are out to find justice... and their mates.

The Detyen Warriors series brings you kick butt heroines, alpha alien heroes, fated mates, and relationships strong enough to span the galaxy!
The entire series is also available in audio!

Soulless

Ruthless

Heartless

Faultless

Endless

———

Guarded by the Shifter

Werewolf. Bodyguard. Mate.
The origins of these shifters are shrouded in mystery, but they're determined to protect their mates from any harm that comes their way.
Also available in audio!

Hunting Season

On the Prowl

Stalking Magic

Wolf Cursed

Hungry for the Wolf

Wolf's Temptation

Stealing the Alpha

**The thief takes what she wants, but the alpha
keeps what's his...**

Join shifter thief Mel as she clashes with lion alpha
Luke in an explosive trilogy of two opposites who
can't keep away from one another.

Also available in audio!

The Alpha Heist

Entangled with the Thief

In the Alpha's Bed

Alien Mates: Planet Exile

Guerran is no place for pretty human women. But
these alien heroes will protect their mates!

Also available in audio!

Exile's Hunter

Exile's Adored

Zulir Warrior Mates

Kidnapped humans. Alien Warriors. Electric wings.

The Zulir Warrior Mates series brings you human heroines and heroes abducted from Earth who find love – and wings! – with the alien warriors who rescue them.

Also available in audio!

Synnr's Saint

Synnr's Hope

Synnr's Spark

Synnr's Kiss

Synnr's Ride

———

Dragon Brides

Dragon Princes. Fierce Women. Love.

Fated mates, fierce women, and dragon princes are ready to find their mates.

Crux

Ranger

Saber

Cipher

Storm

Drake

Asher

Knox

Flint

Alien Holiday Romance

Christmas... in space????
These alien holiday romances look beyond Earth's winter holidays and ring in the season across the galaxy!
Select titles available in audio.
Snowed in with the Alien Beast
The Alien's Winter Gift
The Alien Reindeer's Wild Ride
Trapped with her Alien Mate

Alien Outlaws

Outlaws, schemes, and love... it's all there in the Alien Outlaws series...

Andie Munster is sick of life on Ixilta, the planet she got dumped on after being abducted from Earth six years ago. And when the mysterious and dangerous Xandr shows up looking for a way off the planet, she's half-prisoner, half-co-conspirator in a wild rush to escape.

Rogue Alien's Escape
Rogue Alien's Woman
Rogue Alien's Secret
Rogue Alien's Legacy

———

Find more by Kate Rudolph at www. katerudolph.net

ABOUT KATE RUDOLPH

Kate Rudolph is a paranormal and sci-fi romance writer who lives in Indiana. She loves writing about kick butt heroines and the steamy heroes who love them. She's been devouring romance novels since she was too young to be reading them and had to hide her books so no one would take them away. She couldn't imagine a better job in this world than writing romances and sharing them with her fellow readers.

If you enjoyed this story, please consider leaving a review.

www.ingramcontent.com/pod-product-compliance
Lightning Source LLC
Chambersburg PA
CBHW061812190726
48289CB00007B/2171